Blackbone 4

-A Novel Written by-
Caryn Lee

Copyright © 2015 by True Glory Publications
Published by True Glory Publications LLC

Facebook: Caryn Lee
Twitter: @CarynDLee
Instagram: @authorcarynlee

This novel is a work of fiction. Any resemblances to actual events, real people, living or dead, organizations, establishments or locales are products of the author's imagination. Other names, characters, places, and incidents are used fictitiously.

Cover Design: Michael Horne
Editor: Kylar Bradshaw

Acknowledgments

It's that time again to give thanks to everyone who has encouraged me, supported me, and who has inspired me. First and foremost, I would like to thank God for everything. It's not easy writing and completing a book series. Throughout all the obstacles during the year, I still managed to write and remained focused. Without him, I could not have did it. Secondly, I would like to thank all the readers who have encouraged and supported me since the beginning, who have reached out to me, and who kept asking for more. I would like to say, THANK YOU! You have no idea how much you have played a big part. Thank you for falling in love with my characters and my books. I would also like to thank my family and friends as well. A big thanks to those who have shared to others about my books. Last but not least, thank you to those who have inspired me. There's so many to name and a few don't even realize that they have inspired me. Thank you for all your advice and feedback. I really appreciate all the love and support from everyone. Please enjoy 'Blackbone 4' the last of novel of the book series. It's been a blast and I'm only getting started. I have plenty more drama to bring you in my new novels. Thank You! Thank You! Thank You!

Table of Contents

Blackbone 4

Written By:

Caryn Lee

Chapter One

Smooth

Ring, Ring, Ring.

It was 5:30 a.m. and my cell was ringing. I grabbed my phone rubbing my sleepy eyes to see who it was. My mother's name and number popped up on the screen. I answered quickly.

"Hello, is everything fine Ma?" I asked.

"Eric, she had the baby. I just got off the phone with DCFS and they need me to pick up the baby from Cook County Hospital." She said.

"Okay fine I will meet you there. I'm about to get up now." I said.

I looked over at Ciara who was sleeping. I laid there and stared up at the ceiling. *Damn,* I thought to myself. I wasn't ready for this. I mean, I knew that Kayla was due to have my baby soon, but I wasn't prepared to go over this again with Ciara. I hopped out of the bed without waking Ciara and threw on my jogging suit. I rode to the hospital in silence and made it there by 6:25 a.m. My phone rang and it was Ciara calling me. I thought about answering the phone or not. After the fourth ring, I answered.

"Hello, yeah baby." I said.

"Don't yeah baby me! Where are you?!" Ciara asked.

"I'm at the hospital with my mom." I said.

"The hospital? What's wrong with your mom? Where are you? Why didn't you wake me up, Smooth?" Ciara asked.

"It's fine baby. She wasn't feeling to well and she went to the emergency room. I didn't want to wake you or the kids. I just got here and I'm about to go in and see what's going on now. I will call you back once I find out what's going on." I said.

"Okay. I hope everything is fine. Call me once you find out." Ciara said.

"Cool. I will baby and I love you." I said.

"I love you too, Smooth." Ciara said.

I walked inside the hospital and checked in at the front desk. The lady at the desk gave me a pass and I got on the elevator and went up to the maternity ward. When I arrived, I seen my mother sitting down talking to another woman. She was Caucasian and I assumed that she was the caseworker. I approached them both.

"I'm finally here. Is everything cool?" I asked.

"Hello, I'm Mrs. Peterson the caseworker for Kayla. I take it that you are the father of the newborn baby girl, Variyah Jackson.

"Yes, I'm Eric Jackson."

"Great, I will have you sign the paperwork and after that the baby will be released in your custody."

Mrs. Peterson stood up. "You both can follow me so that we could have some privacy."

My mother and I walked behind her and entered inside a tiny room with a table. On the table was a folder with Kayla's picture and information on it. I looked at the picture for a minute because it has been a while since I've seen Kayla. I signed the paperwork and my mother sat in silence. After I was done, Mrs. Peterson left us alone and went to go get my daughter. Once she was gone my mother spoke.

"Eric have you told Ciara about your baby?" My mother asked.

"Not yet but I plan on telling her soon." I said.

My mother shook her head. "You better tell her or else I will. I don't feel comfortable keeping this away from her. Besides, I don't want to be caught up in all the mess!"

"I know mom. I will tell her but first I have to take a DNA test. I just want to make sure that the baby is mine." I said.

"Eric, you know that the baby is yours. Don't start that craziness but it's your life and if you insist on getting a DNA test that is your business."

I could tell by the look on my mom's face that she was getting tired of the entire mess. She was right about the baby being mine but I just didn't want to believe it. Moments later Mrs. Peterson walked back inside the room carrying my baby girl. She was sleeping and wrapped up in the hospital blanket. I took her into my arms, looked at her, and my heart melted instantly. The caseworker spoke but I tuned her out as I went to inspect her body. Wow she was a splitting image of me. As a matter of fact all my children were. My mother tapped me on the shoulder as I read the wrist band on her arm that said, Variyah Jackson.

"Eric, did you hear a word that she said?" My mother asked.

"No I didn't, may you repeat what you said?" I asked.

"Are they any questions that you have that you would like to ask?" Mrs. Peterson asked.

"Yes. I need information on getting a DNA test. How would I go about doing that?"

"Is there any doubt that you may not be the father? Because if so that would another matter." She responded.

My mother spoke up. "No there isn't any doubt. We are sure that he's the father. Thank you for everything and we will be on our way.

The ride back to my mother's house was a quiet one. I rode in silence, no music all I heard were the thoughts that were inside my head. My mother felt that it was best if baby Variyah rode home with her instead. I agreed because I still couldn't grasp the fact that I had created another child not with the woman that I loved. It was a struggle for me to be the best man for Ciara. I truly love her, although I have a funny way of showing it. My penis on the other hand had a mind of its own. It isn't a day that goes by that I wish that I could turn back the hands of time and do a lot of things different. But fuck it, I can't and I just would have to handle the situation in an adult way. Once we made it back to my mother's house I spent some time bonding with Variyah. Although she looked like me I made arrangements in getting a DNA test performed first thing in the morning. My mother felt that I was being foolish. I felt that I wanted to know 100 percent if Variyah was my daughter. Ciara called my phone several times but I didn't answer. Right now, I was making sure that my mom was straight and that she had everything in order. I was prepared for this day so I had purchased baby items ahead of time. My old bedroom, which was now Variyah's room, was waiting on her arrival. Inside was a mahogany crib, dresser, and changing table set. I also had a rocking chair for when my mother wanted to sit and rock her. Plus diapers stocked with baby essentials and plenty of clothes. My mother placed Variyah inside her crib and she was sleeping, lying on her side. Every time that my mother would place the blanket over her she would remove it. We both laughed because she did it several times and the last time she frowned.

"Well, I know where she gets her ways from. You did the same thing when you were a baby. I will cover you up and when I check on you the blanket would be off you." My mother laughed and said.

"She's going to be a tough cookie I see." I looked at her and stroked her curly black hair. She had a head full of hair just like Erica and Junior had when they were first born. Her skin was brown and she had thick brows similar to mine.

"She's a splitting image of you."

"Yes indeed, she is and I want to thank you for being here for me again. I know that I keep getting myself caught in these predicaments, but I promise not anymore after this. I'm thinking about having a vasectomy." I laughed, but I was so damn serious.

"Son, you don't need to do all that. What you need to do is focus on your family, meaning the woman you love and that is Ciara. You also have to put yourself in her shoes. How would you feel if she was running around behind your back and ended up pregnant by another man? I know that you wouldn't be pleased at all. The things you are doing have consequences. Besides that the things that you do on the outside effects those at home. How are you going to explain to your children as well that they have another sister that didn't come from their mother? What you need to do is grow up and get your life in order before you end up out here with children here, there, and everywhere. I raised and taught you better than all this Eric."

I didn't talk back I just listened. She was right about everything but hey shit happens. I know one mother fucking thing and that was I wasn't having any more children, not unless it was with Ciara. And that is if Ciara doesn't leave me. I left the room, took a seat, and called Red, Ant, and Vell too tell them that Kayla had the baby. Even though each of them were dealing with their own situations, they still supported me. It is what it is, they each congratulated me and couldn't wait to see her. I trusted them all and I know Aaliyah would never run her mouth to Ciara because they didn't really get along. After I ended the call with them, Kayla called me.

"What's up Kayla?"

"Hey, how's my princess doing?"

"Right now, she's asleep in her crib. I've been bonding with her all morning. She's beautiful and looks just like me. My mother has already fallen in love with her."

"Hmmm, okay. Well if she looks just like you, why would you questioned if you were her father, Smooth?! Yes you heard me! The case worker told me how you asked for a DNA test. Smooth don't play with me and insult me like that again! Especially when you and I both know the truth that when we were having sex and that you wasn't using a condom."

"Kayla, you called me to argue? Because if you did I don't have time for the bullshit. I get a DNA on all my children. Variyah is no exception to the rule. Fuck what you talking about and you better watch your tone. You forgot who you talking to, I see."

"You lying but okay cool, you can do the DNA. I'm more than 100% sure that you are the father. Talking about you get a DNA test on all your children, a whole lie. I bet you that you didn't get one on Eric Junior."

"No I didn't because I trust my woman. Ciara isn't trifling like you or Rochelle."

"You know what Smooth I'm going to pretend that I didn't hear you say that. Right now, I'm supposed to be happy that I had a healthy baby girl. Tell your mother hello and I appreciate her for keeping my baby until I get on my feet. Another thing Smooth, you better not have my daughter around Ciara either. I swear if I find out that you do I will break out of here and come fuck you straight up!"

"You sound goofy as hell right now. You worried about all the wrong shit. First place you don't tell me what the fuck to do with our daughter. Second why in the fuck would I have her around Ciara in the first place? She doesn't know anything about you being pregnant or about the baby. I expect to keep it the way."

"What do you mean she doesn't know about Variyah?! So, what you plan on keeping us both a secret?! You plan on keeping us hid forever? Ha! Ha! Ha! Smooth, I thought you would have changed by now and stepped up and became a man. Ha! Ha! Ha! But I guess something's will never change." Kayla chuckled.

"You better watch who you talking to Kayla. You already skating on thin ice!"

"No Smooth, you the one who sliding and skating all around this bitch! Arrrrgh! Omg!" Kayla let out a light scream. "All this is starting to stress me out. I just felt a sharp pain down in my pelvic area. I'm going to end this call and get me some rest. Kiss my baby girl for me and tell her that I love her. Can you also tell your mom that I said thank you for raising my baby until I come home? I will give you a call back a little later. I'm about to pop this pain medication and get some rest."

"Wait grab a pen and some paper and write my mother's number down. That a way you can call her directly to check on Variyah. You ready? The number is 708-555-5555. Cool get you some rest and I'll holler at you later."

I hung up the phone on Kayla's crazy ass. She was getting on my fucking nerves already. I hope I wasn't dealing with another Rochelle because if I was I would hate to have to bury her ass too. I wasn't going through that bullshit all over again. My head was beginning to hurt, that's when I realized that I haven't had anything to eat. My phone rang again and I looked down at the screen and noticed that it was Ciara calling this time. "Damn!" I cursed under my breath, holding the side of my head. I forgot to call her back. I answered and prepared to hear the tongue lashing that she was about to give me. When I answered the phone to my surprise Ciara didn't sound mad at all.

"Hey babe, how is your mother doing?"

"She's fine baby. Her blood pressure was high, once they got it back down the doctor released her. She's in the bed resting right now."

"That's good, I'm happy that she's feeling better. I will give her a call later on this evening. I don't want to disturb her now. When are you coming home? The children are driving me crazy, you hear them in the background asking for you?"

I could hear Erica and Eric Jr. in the background. Erica was the first to get on the phone.

"Daddy! Daddy! Where are you? When I woke up you were gone. I want some pancakes and mommy don't know how to make them like you. She burned them daddy." Erica whined.

I laughed because she was too grown for her own good. She right about Ciara though, she can't make pancakes for nothing in the world.

"Baby girl, I'm on my way home and guess what."

"What daddy?"

"I will bring you and your brother some pancakes."
I said.

"Yes! Daddy said he's bring us some pancakes!"
Erica told both Ciara and her little brother.

Ciara got back on the phone. "You need to hurry up
back home. You left out here to early Smooth."

Before she could piss me off, I cut her off. "Ciara
I'm on my way home now. Let me kiss my mother before I
go. Call in and place the order at IHOP and I will pick it up
on my way home. I love you."

"Okay. I love you too, Smooth."

Before leaving my mother's house, I had a talk with
her. You know that she wasn't letting me leave without
giving me a tongue lashing. I listened to every word and
promised her that I will come clean with Ciara about
everything. I kissed her and told her that Kayla has her
number and will give her a call.

Riding down North Avenue on my way to IHOP, I
noticed two guys driving in a white jeep following me
closely. I grabbed my piece just in case I had to put that
muther fucker to work. I watched them and once they
noticed that I peeped them, they jumped into the left lane
and rode on the side of me. I kept my eyes on them, drove
with my left hand, and had my gun in my right hand. One
of the guys had a mean mug on his face as he stared at me.
I held my gun up and smiled at that clown ass nigga. He

looked at his partner; the driver, and they both nodded their heads. They flew through the yellow light and kept on going. I made a right into IHOP parking lot and whipped into a parking spot. I pulled out my cell to call Red.

"Yo man two niggas in a white jeep was following me down North Ave."

"Where you at right now?" Red asked.

"At IHOP on North Avenue and 10th picking up some food."

"Alright I'm on my way up there, riding down on you now."

"Aye man I'm cool you don't have to come. I ain't worried about them niggas. I just wanted to let you know what the fuck was going on."

"If you straight then its fine with me but I don't have any problem with coming through and making some noise."

"Yeah I'm cool, let me go in here and grab this food. I'll hit you back when I make it home."

"Straight and hit my line if you need me."

I grabbed the food and jumped back in the car. As I drove down the street, I kept my eyes opened and wondered who the fuck those niggas was. You know we were getting a lot more money now and the hungry ones were starting to notice. I'll be damn if I let another nigga take anything that I worked hard for. I didn't keep much cash on me, just enough on me to get a few things. On the way home I drove in silence thinking about my next move.

Kayla

Smooth makes me so damn sick. If he was in front of me right now, I would smack his ass a couple of times. I inhaled and exhaled for a moment and got back to reality. I'm not even going to let him upset me right now or pretty much anymore. I pressed the call light. The nurse stepped in and I asked her for my pain medication. Five minutes later she came back with some fresh water and my pills. I popped them both and swallowed them down with water. Sitting outside my door was a female police officer. She was reading a magazine and wasn't paying me any attention. I was happy that she gave me my privacy. The previous officer that I had before her sat inside the room. It wasn't as if I could run off, one of my arms were hand cuffed to the damn bed. I turned on the television and noticed that a marathon of Snapped was on. I watched my favorite show, two hours had gone by, and my lunch tray had arrived. They served me some dry baked chicken, runny mashed potatoes, and dry ass broccoli. The only thing that I really wanted was the piece of chocolate cake and the can of Sprite. I quickly swallowed the food down and stopped complaining. It was much better than the food in the Fed Joint. After I finished eating, I decided to call my girl Aaliyah to vent and get a few things off my chest. I was still feeling some type of way about the phone call that Smooth and I had. I needed someone to vent too. I picked up the phone and dialed her number.

"Hello Aaliyah." I said dry as hell into the phone.

both know that he is the baby father. Although I can understand where he's coming from." Aaliyah said.

"I can't wait to get released. I'm not hiding shit from no one! If Ciara and I bump into one another and I have Variyah with me, I promise I will make it my business to let her ass know that she is Smooth's daughter!" I said.

"Girl, you're crazy, but that's why I fuck with you! We both crazy but anyway don't let him steal your joy. You just had a healthy baby girl and that's a blessing. Get you some rest and don't let him get you all worked up. In due time you'll be home. Knock that time out and if necessary deal with that mess when you get home. I won't let him upset me if I was you. That's his problem and not yours. He the one who has to deal with Ciara and not you!" said Aaliyah.

"You're right let me calm down and save all my energy for when I get out. Besides it's me and my baby girl against the world. Fuck Smooth and Ciara's situation! As long as he take care of mine, we don't have a problem." I said.

"Yes that is the only thing that really matters. Variyah is the only person that matters at this moment. Well Kayla, I hate to have to end this phone call but I have to get prepared to leave out."

"Bitch, where you about to go?!" I asked being nosy.

"Vell and I are going on a double date with Red and Denise at Uncle Julio's," said Aaliyah.

"Hey what's up boo? I heard the news, Congratulations!!! I can't wait till I see my god daughter. Miss Variyah. I bet she's pretty as can be." Aaliyah said sounding all cheerful and shit.

"Thank you and yes she's gorgeous. She looks just like her hoe ass daddy!"

"Oh shit! What's wrong, Kayla? Did you and Smooth get into it again?" Aaliyah asked.

"You know how we do, I talk crazy and then he tries to check me. Not this time friend! I stood up for myself and kept it real with him. I don't appreciate him keeping Variyah a secret from Ciara. He kept me a secret for so long but he wasn't going to keep my daughter one. You would think after all that I've been through with him that he would fucking tell her!"

"Friend, you sound crazy right now. How do you expect him to tell his main chick, let me correct that, his wife, that he got his side chick that's doing time for him pregnant?! Trust and believe the way he going about doing it is going to get him caught up any way. I can't see him and his mother keeping a secret like that on the hush for too long." Aaliyah said making a valid point.

"Not only that but he had the nerve to say that he's getting a DNA test. That pissed me the fuck off. Girl, I will never be a fool and get pregnant by another man. I've been chasing Smooth for too long. Besides I love him too much to give my pussy away to another man."

"Wow! That's a low blow right there. At least yo don't have to worry about him not being the father. We

"I hope that you don't be running your mouth about me to her. I don't trust her because she's friends with Ciara and Kelly."

"What I look like discussing about you to Denise?! She doesn't even know who you are or that you even exist. Besides she's cool and I like hanging out with her. You know Vell and Red have always been the closer of the two in the group. It feels good finally being able to click with one of Red's girlfriends. You know how he had so many in the past." Aaliyah said.

"Can you try to get some information on Ciara out of her?" I asked being messy.

"Oh that's not going to happen boo. I already tried that move and she isn't talking or giving up the dirt on those two."

"I know her type and I don't trust her. I honestly feel that her loyalty is to Ciara, but hey that's your friend. That's your girl and that's your business as long as my name isn't involved."

It was a moment of silence before Aaliyah spoke again. "To be honest she's actually closer to Kelly than Ciara. You know that I can't stand that bitch, Kelly. Girl lately she's been in good spirits. Maybe because she's getting married soon."

"I forgot about her and Ant getting married soon. Are you going to be a bridesmaid? Ha! Ha! Ha!" I asked laughing.

"Laughing my ass off! Kayla I'm about to end this call because I see that you have hella jokes. The good thing is you're laughing again. I have to go, talk to you later chick." Aaliyah said.

"Good bye and enjoy your dinner date." I said before hanging up.

I was laughing at our conversation. Every time I chat with Aaliyah she makes me laugh. I'm not going to lie I was a little bit jealous because she was hanging out with Denise. Aaliyah is my girl and like a sister to me. The fact that Denise is friends with my enemy rubs me the wrong type of way. I trust Aaliyah and besides Vell wouldn't allow that type of drama and bullshit in his life. When I get out, I'm going to stay in my lane, sit back, and watch all of them. I do not want to kick a bitch ass but if anyone start some shit so be it. The Snapped marathon was still on and I caught a part of the episode when a woman snapped out and stabbed her cheating husband twenty two times because she found out not only was he cheating but he also had another child with the other woman. *Damn,* I thought to myself how similar Smooth and I situation was similar. These some crazy bitches out here and I was one of them. The medication and food was starting to kick in and making me sleepy. I was beginning to drift off to sleep for a nap. I will call to check on my baby girl once I get up.

Two hours later, I woke up and two female officers were posted outside my door. I didn't know what was going on. My only main concern was calling to check on my baby girl. When I moved around to sit up, I got both of their attention. The tall slimmer one only spoke as they both entered my room.

"We will be transporting you back shortly."

16

I simply said okay and asked if I still had time to shower and make a few phone calls. It was approved, so first I went to freshen up and after I was done I called Ms. Jackson to check on my princess. The phone rang twice and Smooth's mom answered the phone.

"Hello Ms. Jackson, how are you doing? I hope that my princess isn't giving you too much trouble," I said.

"Hello Kayla and oh no she's no problem at all. Right now I'm feeding her. How are you doing? Is everything fine?"

"Everything is fine. I'm going back in today, but before I go I would like to speak too my baby girl if you don't mind putting the phone to her ear," Ms. Jackson placed the phone to her ear. I could hear Variyah sucking on the bottle. I spoke into the phone softly not wanting to alarm her.

"Hey mama's princess. How's my princess doing? I miss you so much pretty. I love you princess and I will see you soon. Kiss, kiss and I love you, Variyah. I love you so much."

I heard baby sounds and I smiled into the phone. She was trying to reply back to me. Ms. Jackson got back on the phone. "She's looking all around for you. Now she's looking at me and smiling."

A tear rolled down my face. I didn't want to cry and breakdown on the phone. Ms. Jackson could hear my voice starting to crack. She assured me not to worry about anything and promise to bring her after a few weeks to visit me. After I heard that, I felt better leaving Variyah with Ms. Jackson. I thanked her for everything and hung up to call Smooth. When I called him, he didn't answer. I called back two more times and still didn't get an answer. I felt like he was avoiding my phone call because he was well aware of Cook County Hospital number. It hurt inside but I laughed it off and didn't let it get to me. Sometimes you have to laugh to keep from crying. Moments later my nurse walked in with my discharge instructions and medications. I signed the paperwork and it was right back to reality. The cold rain hit my body as I climbed inside the van. It was a short, quick ride back but I tried my best to mentally prepare myself for this moment. My first childbirth experience was bitter and sweet. Being incarcerated for my entire pregnancy and having my child while one hand was cuffed to the rail was the bitter part. Having a healthy and beautiful baby girl that had a responsible father was the sweet part. All that mentally trying to stay strong shit went right out the window. I broke down once I made it back to my cell. My very first pregnancy and I'm serving time for a man that doesn't even care enough to answer when I call. A man who isn't in love with me and has a wife and family that comes first. A man that I would give my all to. How in the hell did I get caught in this situation? How silly of me to think I could ever replace Rochelle or ever take Ciara's place. Cherish walked in and I didn't even acknowledge her presence. I simply ignored her and continued crying.

"Kayla, what is the matter? Why are you crying?" Cherish asked.

I fell into Cherish's arms and let it all out. I felt like she was the only one that I could trust at the moment. She removed my hair from my face and looked me in my eyes.

"Let it all out, it's better that way instead of keeping it all inside. Trust me, I know how you feel being that I just

18

went through the same thing. It's very hard giving birth and leaving your baby after you have carried her inside you for nine months. Pretty soon it will be all over and we will be reunited with our babies."

I cried but managed to speak. "Why Smooth don't love me? I just gave birth to his daughter and he still doesn't love me. I'm sitting in jail, no visits and not even a fucking card. He doesn't care about me and never will. He controls everything, why does he have so much power over me?" I cried.

Cherish looked at me with a disgusting look upon her face. From the look on her face, she was ready to check me and go off. Before she spoke, her face softened up a bit not wanting to hurt my feelings.

"Girl, look I'm just going to keep it real with you because I like you and we've grown to become friends. This man has control over you because you allow him to. So stop all that damn crying. Now is the time to get on your business. You know you have a few months to go and you'll be free. The only thing that you should be thinking about is your next move and not be worried about no damn man. Especially a man who has another family."

I looked at Cherish in shock. How did she know about Smooth having another family? I didn't tell her about that part of the drama. I was thinking but she interrupted my train of thought.

"Yes honey I know all about your boyfriend and the situation that you got yourself in. What you thought I wasn't going to do a background check on you? Ha! You do recall the reason why I'm locked up in here right?"

I completely stopped crying as I wiped the tears from my face. In the back of my mind, I was wondering how much Cherish had known. I also wondered if this was going to affect our friendship. She looked at me and continued to talk answering my question.

"Hey, you still cool with me. I'm the last person to pass judgment on anyone. I do commend you on doing his time because you could've have ran your mouth. You a real down ass loyal side chick but you are weak Kayla. You are easy to mislead and controlled by the dick. I don't know what is so special about his, but you can kiss that dream of you and him living happily ever after together fairytale goodbye. What you need to be doing is focusing on what you plan on doing once you step out of here. Have you thought about that? What exactly are your plans?"

Damn she certainly keep it real with me and I'm not upset or even mad for her keeping real. Right now, I didn't know what the hell I was going to do once I was released. "I really don't have any plans. I was depending on Smooth to look out for me," I said.

"See that's the problem right there because basically without him you have nothing. Don't get me wrong he supposed to make shit right once you get out. But it's nothing like making your own money. I can help you out if you serious about making your own money," said Cherish.

Hearing the word money made me excited. "I'm all about making money, after all it's about Variyah now. I can't be out here broke with a baby on my hip."

"Cool. I will teach you how to create checks and crack cards. I get out ahead of you and I will have everything rolling by the time you get out. If you follow instructions very well and learn very quickly, money will never be an issue for you. I can't go into details about everything right now but just know that Cherish is about making her money. Love is cool but it doesn't pay no bills or buy you all the luxury things in life. Besides don't nobody have time for all that man drama, you can apply all that energy into making money. Shake that shit off girl. You are someone's mother now and you and the baby can't be crying. You really are going to run Smooth off by doing that. Woman up and stop being a drama queen, don't nobody have time for that!"

"Well damn thanks for keeping it real with me because I was losing it. I just need to not let him get to me. It's hard when you have feelings for someone and want him so bad. I'm just going to take it one day at a time and I need your help with getting him out of my system. He's like a lighter to my cigarette. Girl, I can't cope without him and I came so close to losing him so many times that I've lost count. I feel like now that I have his child that I'm in his life forever. We have a bond that can't be broken. You know I finally got him trapped now. I know it's not right that I feel that way but it's partially true. I'm still hoping that everything change for the best when I get out. I just had a moment and got caught in my feelings." I said.

"You know I'm going to keep it real with you because being real is the only thing that I know. Get yourself back together in here and once you step out this place show him how much that you have changed. Take charge and control of your life. I'm not saying that you have to stop checking paper from him. I'm saying that whatever he gives you should be extra and not the only thing that you depend on. What if something happens to him? You can kiss that income goodbye. I'm not trying to scare you, I'm trying to prepare you." Cherish said.

I took heed on everything that she was saying. From this point on I was taking control of my life. I didn't care what the next person said, my goal is to become Smooth's girl. Ciara has to go!

Ciara

Lately things at home have been going great. Smooth has transformed back into the man that I fell in love with. He has been spending more time with me and the children and participating in family activities. I don't know why the sudden change but I can tell you one thing and that is, I'm not going to complain. Although things have been great at home, I still managed to creep off with Kanye. I know it's so wrong but I just can't shake him. When I'm with him, I feel free. No screaming children, no work, and no drama. During my free time I would run off with Kanye and just be myself. He didn't like sharing me with Smooth, his goal was take me away and win my heart. It felt weird seeing two men, Smooth has been the only man that I've been with. I wasn't going to cross that line with Kanye. No sex was a strict rule for me, besides he didn't pressure me about it, which lead me to think if he was screwing another woman. I didn't know and to be honest I didn't want to know. Right now it felt good having two men catering to me. I had a street man and a working man. Best of both worlds and I'm enjoying every moment.

It was a rainy weekend and London was at the boutique today running things. My mother had the children for the weekend. Smooth and I were in the house exploring one another's body. He softly kissed me from head to toe not missing a spot. His tongue took over making my eyes roll to the back of my head. I loved and hated when he gave me his awesome head. Loved it because he made me feel good. Hated it because I felt that every time the sex was amazing that something was going on. Smooth has been acting kind of strange lately. Every time I left the house he needed to know every move that I made. That didn't rest well with me as a matter of fact it was getting on my nerves. Moments after he was done devouring me, Smooth laid down beside me. I tongue kissed him tasting my sweet juices. I felt refreshed all over again. I rested my head on his chocolate chest. Closed my eyes and enjoying the quietness. He broke the silence in the room.

"Baby, you know that I love you right," Smooth said kissing me softly on my forehead.

"Yes babe and I love you too. For some reason why do I feel like something is going on," I said with my eyes remaining closed.

Smooth's heart began to race. "Nothing is going on, I just wanted to tell you that I love you."

I could feel his heart beating rapidly as he lied to me. I don't know what the hell was going on, but I was about to find out exactly what he was keeping from me. I sat up and looked into his eyes slightly raising my voice and said, "Eric what the hell is going on?!"

He looked at me with uneasy look in his eyes and tried to kiss me again. I stopped that kiss with my index finger. I didn't have time for that kissy shit. Smooth remained quiet and that really pissed me off but I remained calm. Acting out will never get the information that I needed.

"Talk!" I said

Smooth avoided eye contact with me before speaking. It made me worry about what he was about to say. Whatever it was, I was ready to hear it.

"Check it out, for the past two weeks there's been some people following me. Before you start worrying about anything, we found out who they are. Everything will be handled properly."

"That's why you have been acting so strange. Asking me my whereabouts and what not? Calling me every 15 minutes checking on me. Babe, you could've told me what was going on." I said getting out of the bed and grabbing my Chanel bag. I reached inside and pulled out my baby 380. Smooth's eyes widen when he noticed that I had a new piece. "When and where did you get that baby?" he asked.

"I upgraded when my boutique was mysteriously burned down. I looked at the gun admiring it as if it was a new pair of shoes or a new hand bag. Isn't it pretty? It fits me perfectly." I aimed the gun at our bedroom wall pretending to fire several shots. The safety was on so it was no need to worry.

"Blackbone, I don't want you out here shooting people and shit. That's my job, you let me handle all of that. Put that gun down and get over here and take care of daddy."

I looked over and seen that Smooth had a standing ovation. My pussy jumped and I immediately put away the gun and made my way over to Smooth. Straddling him, his dick slipped inside me, my perky dark breasts bounced up and down as I rode him. He felt so good inside me that he had me thinking about slowing things down with Kanye.

Monday morning I strolled into my boutique smiling and glowing. "Good morning." I said to London and the two customers that she was ringing up. I didn't have a care in the world. I went to my office in the back room and hung up my jacket. Today I had on a two piece legging set that fit my curves. I walked back out and the customers were no longer there. Looking over at London with a silly smile on her face, I couldn't help but ask her what the hell was she was smiling so hard for.

"What? A girl can't come into work happy and smiling?" I asked jokily.

"Girl bye, you aren't fooling me. I know someone enjoyed their weekend a little too much I see. You come strolling in here all happy and shit. Spill it girl! Please don't leave nothing out." London said.

"Well since you asked, I must say that I did have a good time with the Mr. It feels good that everything is back to normal. No more arguing and fighting. Just laughs and a whole lot of lovemaking. Smooth put it down like he used to. Girl if he keeps it up, I just might stop dealing with Kanye."

"That's good to hear that everything is going well at home. I mean Ciara you and Smooth have been through a lot and I would love to see you two together. Don't get me wrong Kanye is a nice man to have on the side too. Let's not rule him out so fast. I hope that Smooth continues to keep you smiling and finally stop playing games."

"Who you telling because he only has one more chance London. If he fucks up again, I'm leaving this time for real. I will still remain friends with Kanye but I'm not going to sleep with him. Nor lead him on to believe that I'm happy with seeing the both of him and Eric. I must admit it does feel good to know that I have an option. Right now, I'm enjoying my man, I'm happy that he's doing better and starting to take our marriage a lot more serious."

"I know that's right enjoy yourself but be careful and don't let your feelings get involved. It's all fun in games until someone gets hurt. Just be up front with Kanye so that he's aware of everything and won't get hurt. And know what to expect," said London.

"Yes that's the last thing that I want to do is hurt anyone. If only I would've met Kanye first, then I will be his girl for sure. You know I love Smooth but I don't really care for what he does. It's so much that comes along with that lifestyle. Oh well I'm not going to dwell on this anymore. What's going on in here? Anything that I need to know that happened over the weekend?" I asked.

"Sure. I should be getting a new shipment of maxi dresses and sandals in today. On Thursday the sun hats should arrive. We haven't decided on what else you would like to order. Plus, we need to set up model auditions for our summer fashion show." London said.

I soaked all that in and started to get to work. It was so much to get done, it was spring time and summer is just around the corner. All work and no play was my motto. Juggling both Eric and Kanye was taking up too much of my time. Time is money and I had a business to run and money to make. I had to remain focus especially since I'm aware that I have to be safe out here due to the fact that someone is coming for my man. Right now everything is fine but how was I going to stop seeing Kanye. That was going to be the hard part.

Chapter Two

Kanye

I tried several times to reach out to Ciara but she hasn't answered or returned my calls. It's been two weeks since the last I've heard of her. I was too embarrassed to have Jay ask his woman, London, to have Ciara to call me. I was concerned if she was doing fine or not. Although I knew that she had a man, I still wanted her badly. She was perfect, smart, beautiful, and full of life. I was secretly hoping that her man messed up at home and that she would come running back to me. I could tell that things had to be going right and that was the reason why I have not seen or heard from Ciara. I scrolled through the pictures in my phone and looked at the remaining ones that I had of her. Her beautiful dark cocoa brown, flawless skin and bright smile made me miss her even more. Lately, I tried to stay busy and focus on my job duties. A few times I stepped out with a female friend or two to have fun but they didn't compare to Ciara. I would end up back thinking of her. Damn I had to get this woman out of my system. Jay and I went to Hawkeyes and decided to have a few drinks, wings, and watch the Chicago White Sox vs Atlanta Braves game. It was packed inside but we grabbed a table and sat down. The women were deep in here and looking good but not as fine as Ciara. I ordered a few Corona's and some wings. Jay's phone rang and I overheard him talking to London. If I heard him correctly, she was on her way up there to meet him. As soon as he ended his call, I asked him if Ciara was joining her. He answered that he wasn't sure or not. The game started and the White Sox were doing great. I bet Jay that the White Sox were going to beat the Braves ass. Jay was a diehard Atlanta Braves fan and took me on for the bet. We chilled out, knocked some drinks and wings back until halftime. The White Sox were up by 2-0 we were going to win for sure but Jay kept talking mad shit about how the Braves are going to catch up and bragging about B.J. Upton. Jay looked down at his vibrating phone and read a text message that someone had sent him. "London is looking for a parking space." He said as he replied back to the message. "Hell for a minute I forgot that she was coming."

"You just be ready to pay me my money when the Braves lose." I said signaling the waitress over to order more drinks and wings. I still wondered if London had Ciara with her. I told Jay that I was going to take a piss and made my way through the crowded sports bar. When I stepped back out, a young woman along with her friends flirted with me. I flashed a smile being friendly and courteous but I was not interested. With her eyes, she flirted back with me. Jay was laughing loudly and his voice caught my attention. I looked over to see what the hell was going on. There she was standing next to London wearing a White Sox tee shirt and some tight jeans. Her round ass stuck out drawing attention. She had on some black high heels making her seem much taller than she actually was. I watched her smile and give Jay a friendly hug. The flirting woman peeped that she was no longer getting my attention, her eyes darted across the room and landed on Ciara. She quickly glanced back at me and rolled her eyes. I didn't give a fuck my baby was in the building looking good. I walked through the crowd not paying attention to what was going on around me. Only looking straight ahead, Ciara locked eyes with me. Her eyes said I'm sorry. I approached them and spoke to London never once taking my eyes off of Ciara. She looked fresh and beautiful. I stared at her for a moment without saying a word. I know it's been only two weeks but seems so long since I've seen her. She smiled and spoke to me, "Hello Kanye." London and Jay both watched us waiting to see what I was about to say. The game was back on and begun to get louder in the sports bar as people yelled and screamed watching the game. "Can we step outside for a minute?" I asked in hopes that she wouldn't mind. Ciara said yes and we both walked outside. The weather wasn't that bad outside being that it was May in Chicago. We both looked at one another waiting to see who was going to speak first. Both speaking at the same time, "I'm sorry Kanye" Ciara said.

"I miss you Ciara," I said. She looked at me with a sigh of relief. Since she seemed nervous to talk, I went first.

"I'm not upset that I haven't seen or heard from you in two weeks. I don't care about that as long as you're fine. I understand and known up front about your situation so I can't be mad. Ciara, I don't want you to feel as though that you can't talk to me about anything."

"I'm totally sorry about ignoring you. That was immature and childish of me to do. I just didn't know how I was going to tell you that I decided to give my marriage another chance and take it more seriously. It wouldn't be right to continue seeing or talking to you. Kanye, I hope that you understand." Ciara said looking sad with her head down.

I placed my right hand under her chin and lifted her head up. Ciara looked me in my eyes. I grabbed her hands and held them, making her feel comfortable. I looked into her eyes and said, "Baby, I understand and can't do anything but accept the fact that you are working on keeping your family together. You're doing the right thing. Besides, I want you and I could never imagine sharing you with anyone else. I hope that we could remain friends even if you can't be my woman now. You never know what the future holds and I'm not giving up until I get you."

"Kanye it was so hard staying away from you and you talking like this is making it even harder. You are right you don't know what the future holds, but I do know that if and when you and I are together. That I will be your one and only, you deserve the same. We will always remain friends but I'm in love with Eric." Ciara said choking up and beginning to cry.

"Don't cry beautiful," I hugged her. I don't like to see you crying and hurt. She broke away from my hug and ran off quickly.

"Sorry Kanye I have to go. Facing you was a bad idea, tell London that I will call her." She ran off to her car.

"Ciara wait, you don't have to go." I ran after her an older couple was in my way making it hard for me to keep up with her. Ciara made it to her car and jumped inside. I grabbed onto her car door, "Ciara, can I please talk to you?" She sped off into traffic. "Damn!" I said out of breath.

I went to my car and called Jay and told him what had happen and that I was going after Ciara. He understood but advised me to give her a chance to get herself together before I went after her. I went against his advice and decided to go after her anyway. I rode down Western Ave. I knew that she couldn't be too far away. One block up I could see her Lexus in the turning lane and she had her left turning signal on. She turned off onto Harrison. My light turned green and I cut off two cars in front of me to catch up with her. They blew their horns but I didn't give a fuck. I got into the turning lane and made a left turn trying to catch up with her. She jumped on the expressway not knowing that I was behind her. I called her several times following behind her for 15 minutes. She exited off Wolf Rd. riding through Westchester. Slowing down and doing the speed limit allowed Ciara to leave me in the dust. I pulled out my phone and carefully called her again. I noticed a police car sitting on the side of the road. Calling her distracted me and I got caught by a fucking right light. By the time I caught up with her she was pulling up inside a garage. This must be where she lives, her house was nice. Not bad for a hustler but I know that I could do better if she only would let me. I hit her with a text message: I'm outside your house.

Sitting back watching her home, I seen Ciara peep out of her blinds. She rushed outside furious looking back over her shoulder making sure that anyone had not seen her. I'm not going to lie seeing her mad right now made me regret following her. I've never seen her so upset. She jumped inside my car.

"Are you crazy?! I can't believe that you followed me to my home! This is so creepy! Oh my God if Eric catches you here it won't be nice!" Ciara said looking over her shoulder.

"We need to finish our talk Ciara. I wasn't going to let you run off this time and get away from me. I know that this is creepy but I love you."

"You love me?" She chuckled. "Kanye please leave before Eric see the both of us! If you love me right now, you will let me free and let me be."

I grabbed her forcefully and kissed her. She punched me several times trying to stop me. I continued to kiss her and she bit my lip. "Shit!" I cursed rubbing my bottom lip. "Why did you do that?!"

She ignored me trying to get out the car. "Kanye unlock your doors please and let me out!" she demanded.

"Not until you listen to me, can you please calm down. Look, I don't want to lose you. I know that you have a family and everything that you're fighting to keep together but that man doesn't truly love you. He can't love you like I love you. Any man that cares about you would have never had a child by another woman first and then try to hide it. He wouldn't have you drinking and losing yourself."

Smack! Ciara slapped me across my face. "Shut up Kanye you don't have the right to go there! He does love me and he apologized several times!" She cried with tears running down her face.

"I can love you better Ciara and I will." She looked at me. For a moment I thought that she was going to slap me again. Instead she kissed me deeply with so much passion. When she stopped, we both looked at one another.

"Kanye, I can't help that I'm in love with him and you. I have a family and I'm thinking about them. It would be selfish of me to drag them along in this mess. Please just give me some time, I promise that I won't run off again. I have to go now before someone sees us."

Ciara got out of the car and quickly ran back to her house. Before she stepped inside, she looked back at me, signaling for me to go. I noticed a guy in a white Benz pull up in front of her garage. I pulled off leaving Ciara's house and never looking back.

Kelly

"Girl, no he didn't follow you home. Oh wow, that is all too much for me to take in right now. What are you going to do friend?" I asked Ciara as she was sitting across from me at my dining room table.

"Kelly, I don't know, I'm so confused. We both know that Smooth hasn't been the best but I love him. Girl, I was pissed when he said that bullshit about his past and bringing up Rochelle. Talking about he could love me better, that's so easier to say when you are the other man." Ciara said.

"Yes that was wrong for him to go there. That was funny that you slapped him. Girl, I would've did the same. Ciara, you didn't sleep with him yet have you?" I asked her being serious.

"Kelly, I've never gave him the pussy. Kanye hasn't even seen me naked before. You know that I wouldn't lie to you about that."

"I'm just asking because I'm just trying to figure out why he just doesn't move on. I don't know what to tell you being that I've never been in this situation before.

Whatever you decide to do, I will support you and have your back." I said.

"Girl, I know you do that's why I love you. Okay enough of my bullshit. What's going on with you and Ant? You two love birds, look at you blushing when I say his name." Ciara said teasing me.

"That's my hubby, everything is all good. We just planning our wedding, well correction, I'm planning it. Ant said that he doesn't care what I do that's my day. I'm looking for a wedding planner. GG was trying to get me to hire some older lady that goes to her church. I told her that I will keep her in mind but just to make her happy."

"Right, we need someone who's popping and younger. Well, I'm so excited for the both of you. I can not wait for that day to come. You two deserve to be together." Ciara said.

I could tell that she was starting to look sad so I changed the subject cutting her off. "Ciara, come here. I have to show you something. Follow me." I said walking down my hallway to my bedroom.

Ciara followed behind me, "Girl what you about to show me?" she laughed and asked. I opened up my bedroom door to show her that I had installed a stripper pole.

"Kelly gone girl! So when did you get it?" Ciara asked.

"Last week and haven't used it yet because I don't have a trick to use. I've been meaning to call Tia so that she can train me." I said laughing.

"As a matter of fact let me call Tia' crazy ass. She's been calling me like crazy but every time she calls I'm either too busy to talk or not alone. Let me face time her." Ciara pulled out her iPhone and called up Tia. Tia's face popped up on her screen. "Hey Tia bitch!" we both said yelling into the phone.

"Hey bitches what's up! I'm so glad that you called me because a bitch is in the house bored ass hell." Tia said happily.

"What till you see what Kelly has to show you girl." Ciara turned her phone to show Tia my stripper pole.

Tia screamed into the phone. "Oh shit now!" We all busted out laughing.

"Tia, I need your help girl. I don't have the slightest clue on what to do on this pole. I just got it and I plan on using it for a lifetime." I said.

"You know that I got you and what better moment than now to share my great news. I will be doing my very first set of 'Tia's Teach Me How Too Strip' videos. A production company heard about me and offered me a great deal that I couldn't resist. I start shooting next week, it's going to be a total of ten videos. I'm working bitches, I made it!" Tia said dancing.

"That's great!" Ciara and I was so happy for her. We talked and caught up with everything that was going on in our lives. Tia's birthday was coming up and she and Tommy were going on a trip. She was excited and happy and rambled on and on about it. We laughed so hard when we got off the phone with Tia, every time we talked with her she had a story to tell. Ciara helped me prepare dinner.

We cooked Baked Tilapia, Shrimp, Broccoli, and Corn on the Cobb. Anthony text me saying that he was on his way home. Ciara left shortly because Smooth started blowing her phone up. I freshened up and waited for my hubby to come home. It was 9 pm and an hour ago since he text me. To make time go by I sat on the couch scrolling through my phone on my Facebook page. I have a Facebook and Instagram page but barely have time to be on there. When I logged in, I had multiple notifications, friend requests from people that I don't even know, and 1 message. I clicked on my messages to see who had sent me one, if it was a creep ass dude he was getting cursed out. To my surprise it wasn't a creepy message. It was a shady message from Shunda, the bitch Ebony best friend, who man she fucked as well. She sent this message three weeks ago. *What the hell does she want?* I thought to myself as I read it.

"Hey this is Shunda, if you don't mind can you please give me a call." She left her phone number and I had me thinking what she and I have to talk about. It had to be one reason and that was Ebony. I called her private because I wanted to know what she wanted. She picked up the phone, "Hello." the background was quiet.

"Can I speak to Shunda?" I asked.

"This is Shunda speaking, who is this?" she asked.

"This is Kelly you inbox me and asked me to call." I said with a get straight to the point attitude.

"I thought that you weren't going to call. I reached out to you in regards of the hoe, Ebony. I can't do too much talking over the phone. Would you mind meeting with me someplace so that we could talk in private?" she asked.

"We could meet tomorrow at Mac Arthur's around 1p.m. tomorrow is that fine with you?" I asked.

"Yes. I will meet you there." Shunda said.

Ant keys jingled in the door as he unlocked it. Finally my baby was home! I ran and jumped in his arms causing Ant to drop the duffle bag he was carrying. He hugged and kissed me back, "I miss you babe." I said smothering him with kisses as if he's been gone forever.

"What have you been doing all day beautiful?" Ant asked putting me down.

"Ciara came by to keep me company today. Let me fix your plate." I said walking off to the kitchen. Anthony watched me switch into the kitchen. I was wearing a red lace bra and boy short set. He loved when I wear anything in lace. He went upstairs to shower as I prepared our plates. Anthony left his phones on the dining room table. For the first time, I didn't feel the urge to go through his phones. I trusted my man and knew that he loved me. The old me would've went through his phones and acting a fool. Not anymore that shit is over with and we both have matured. Instead I went over to pick the duffle bag up and unzipped it. I counted the money and placed it neatly in piles of a thousand each. Once I was done it was twenty thousand on the table. Ant came back down stairs wearing a wife beater, pair of boxers, and socks. He placed the money inside the safe. We ate our dinner and I listened as he talked about his day.It was getting late and I can tell by the look in his eyes that he was ready to fuck. I've been ready since he walked through the door. We made our way upstairs and Ant pulled my boy shorts off. I couldn't even get my bra off fast enough before he fucked me to sleep.

The next day I met with Shunda at Mac Arthur's. When I walked in, she was sitting at the table eating alone. I said a short prayer inside my head before I went to join her. "Lord please don't have me in here beating nobody down today, Amen." I made my over to the table and had a seat.

"Hello Kelly, I'm so glad that you could make it. Thank you for coming." Shunda said.

"No problem at all, so what is it that you want to talk about that you couldn't talk about over the phone?" I asked not being friendly nor mean but I did remain calm.

"Look, I could tell by the look on your face that you really don't want to be here. I'm just going to get straight to the point. The reason that I've asked to meet with you was to share some valuable information that can help the both of us."

"What information is that?" I asked.

"You and I both have something in common and that is we both want that whore Ebony dead." Shunda said with vengeance in her eyes.

"It's no secret that you hate that bitch for fucking your man and having his baby. Plus she was involved in Ant's kidnapping. She deserves to die." I said short and sweet.

"You and everyone has already heard my story. My best friend was fucking my man and got pregnant by him, had his child, they both ran off together and lived happily never after. The best part of the story was that he was killed. It allowed me to collect my insurance policy that I had on him." Shunda smiled.

This bitch was crazy I thought to myself. Shunda continued to talk, "Anyway I know where we can find the whore, Ebony. I heard that she was living in Dallas, Texas.

"Really? How sure are you of that?" I asked wanting to know if she will reveal her source.

"A friend of mine is dating her male cousin, Rio. One day she overheard him talking to her on the phone saying that he will visit her soon in Dallas."

"That's a good reliable source. Can your friend get an address on her? You know maybe sneak around through Rio things. Shunda, why are you sharing this information with me? Are you trying to get me to join you? I'm confused." I asked because I was curious and wanted to know.

"Around town I heard that Ebony has a bounty on her head. I really don't care about the money. I hate he bitch so much that i want her dead. When I found out that she was down in Texas I wanted to share that information with you." Shunda said.

I sipped on my glass of water and sized her up. Shunda wasn't a bum bitch, her hair and nails were nice, she had on designer clothes, and a designer bag. This girl was hurt, angry, and all about her money. I can't blame her though. Ebony and Rio made a fool of her so I understand why she wanted revenge. Shunda broke the silence.

"You're not getting anything to eat?"

Getting something to eat wasn't going to happen. I wasn't here to have lunch with a friend. "I had a big breakfast this morning." I said lying.

"Look Kelly, I'm not trying to be your BFF or anything, I just thought that my information could be helpful to Ant. I came to you first only out of respect because I could've just not included you in this at all. Ant is cool and I've never had a problem with him but he's a very hard man to catch up with. We could do this together or separate either way Ebony is going to get what is coming to her." Shunda said looking serious.

I thought before I spoke because I was trying to change for the better. I was tired of talking to her and decided that it was time for me to go. I had better shit to do, like homework instead of talking to her. "It's time for me to go." I said looking at my watch. Before Shunda could say anything else, I was out of my seat and out the front door.

I called Ant once I got inside my car. He answered and I asked where he was at and told him that we needed to talk. Luckily, he was in the house. I walked through the door to find him playing the game. "Babe, I just left from talking with Shunda about Ebony being down in Dallas." I said.

Anthony continued to play his game not looking at me as he spoke. "We know that Ebony is down in Texas. If she finds her before I do, the money is hers."

I sat down next to him and took the game controller out of his hand and paused the game. "Can you please pay attention to me? So all this time you knew where she was?" I asked.

"Yes but no one has confirmed it. We're not sure if she's in Dallas or Houston." He said getting frustrated because I stopped his game. I threw the game controller at him. "Thank you and baby don't worry about Ebony I got that covered." He said kissing me.

I walked off and went to go do my homework. To be honest I wasn't thinking about Ebony and if my man said he would handle it that was fine with me. From this moment on, the only thing I'm concerned about is me walking across the stage and walking down the aisle.

Chapter Three

Aaliyah

I spent my entire morning grocery shopping and buying household products for the house. The girls were in school and Vell was out in the streets. By the time that I made it home it was going on noon. I pulled in my garage and took the bags inside. The house was clean and peaceful. Having a set of twin girls will drive you crazy. I kicked off my shoes and rubbed my feet. I don't know why I went grocery shopping with heels on. I ran the water in my Jacuzzi tub and dialed Vell's number but he didn't pick up. I sent him a text message reminding him not to forget to pick the girls up from school. I got in the water and soaked for about fifteen minutes until my skin started to wrinkle up. Once I got out my phone started ringing, it was Vell calling me back. I answered the phone and said hello but he didn't say anything back. I could hear noise in the background and it sounded like someone was moaning. I sat on my bed listening to my man fucking another bitch. I could hear them both, Vell had the bitch screaming his name. I grabbed my chest checking to see if my heart was still there.

"Whose pussy is this?" Vell asked the girl.

She moaned, "Your pussy daddy."

I couldn't believe what I was hearing. I tried my best to listen but I couldn't take it anymore when I heard Vell say to the female that he loved fucking her raw I busted out yelling.

"Nigga, I can hear your nasty ass!" I screamed into the phone.

44

I heard some rambling going on and the call ended. I called his nasty ass back several times but he didn't answer. I laid out on my bedroom floor naked, crying into his phone leaving him a voice message. I felt the urge to throw up and crawled into the bathroom hovering over the toilet. Everything that I ate came up. It hurt to my stomach to hear my man fucking another female without protection. I got my dumb ass up and rinsed my mouth out and threw on some sweats. Vell was getting fucked up as soon as he made it home. I sat right on my couch and two hours later Vell and the girls walked through the door.

"Mommy, mommy look what we made in school today." the twins said showing me their paintings.

"They look beautiful." I said kissing them both. "Hey can you two go upstairs to your room? Mommy has to talk with daddy, I will be up there when I'm done." I said. The girls ran upstairs to their room.

Vell walked off but I grabbed his arm. "So you going to walk in here like you just didn't get caught fucking another bitch?!"

"I don't know what you're talking about Aaliyah. You ain't catch me doing shit." He walked in the kitchen and grabbed him a bottle of water. I knocked that shit out of his hand.

"Gone Aaliyah I'm not about to do this with the girls in the house."

"We are about to do this now! You know what Vell I don't even know why I'm still even with you! Just get your shit and go! I don't have time for this anymore! You know damn well that I heard you on the phone with your nasty ass! I fucking hate you!" I said and spit in his face.

Smack!

"What the fuck is wrong with you?! Do you ever spit on me again!" Vell yelled. The girls ran to the top of the stairs looking down at us.

"Everything is ok girls please go back into your room." I said.

Vell sat down on the couch and I went into the kitchen to grab a butcher knife. I ran up on him and sliced him several times. "What the fuck is wrong with you?!" I tuned him off and snapped. Stabbing him several times until he grabbed a hold of me and threw me down on the floor. I kicked and screamed, "Don't you ever put your muther fucking hands on me again!"

The twins were crying and screaming for us to stop fighting. Vell grabbed his car keys and ran out the door. His blood was covered all over my body, I was losing it. I ushered the girls upstairs as they continued to cry and sat them in front of the television. "Mommy is fine, everything is fine. Here you go watch Frozen, girls. Mommy has to go and get cleaned up." I said rushing out of their room. I took a look at myself in the full length mirror. "Oh my God what have I done?" I looked like a crazy lady. I got in the shower and scrubbed Vell's blood off of my skin, out of my nails, and out of my hair. I cried hysterically and punched myself in the head several times asking myself, "What have I done?" When I got out I sat on the bed shaking, my phone rang scaring me causing me to jump. It was Niecy calling me I quickly answered, "Hello."

"Aaliyah what the hell is going on?!" asked Niecy.

"I snapped! I snapped! I snapped Niecy!" I said biting my nails and shaking.

"Why? Forget that where are the twins? Please tell me that they're ok!" asked Niecy.

"I snapped, I muther fucking snapped!" I continued to say.

"I'm on my way now, Aaliyah!" Niecy said.

I slipped on a tee shirt and paced my room back and forth calling Vell's phone several times, but I kept getting the voicemail. My door had to be unlocked because Niecy was walking up my stairs holding her chest with a look of panic on her face. She checked on the twins to make sure that they were fine. I sat on my bedroom floor praying to God that Vell was fine and asking for his forgiveness. Niecy walked inside and hugged me. "Aaliyah, are you okay? What happened?" she asked.

"Vell was fucking another bitch. He came home, he hit me, and I went to go get the knife and that's the last thing that I remember." I said talking fast.

"Slow down, slow down, you're talking too fast. You caught Vell fucking another bitch?" she asked.

"He had her screaming his name. He said that he loved fucking her raw." I cried.

"Are you serious? That's not good, that's not good at all." Niecy's phone rang and she answered. From the conversation, I could tell that she was talking to Red about my situation. She told Red that me and the twins were fine and that she was going to stay to help me clean up. I grabbed her phone to talk to Red.

"How is Vell doing?" I asked. But Red had already hung up the phone. Niecy took her phone back from me.

"Vell is doing fine. He's at Loyola getting taking care off. Enough about him, Aaliyah you need to be concerned about you. Right now, you should be on the phone making a doctor appointment. Fuck Vell! He will be okay but what about you? You can't have them poor girls in there seeing all this." Niecy said standing up and waving her arms around. "You and Vell in here acting like animals and shit around them precious girls of yours, traumatizing them for the rest of their lives. There's got to be some changes done and it has to start with you first."

"I didn't mean for all this to happen and to go down the way that it did. It happened so fast and all I remember is seeing red and I snapped! I love my girls, I swear to God that I love my girls!" I said crying.

"I know that you love them, but you have to love yourself. Stop crying it's all over now and I'm here for you. Let me go and check on the twins, I'm sure that they're hungry." Niecy went to go check on the girls and I called my doctor to make an appointment. They were able to squeeze me in two days from now. Niecy went downstairs to cook the girls something to eat, making them some burgers and fries. She helped them with their homework, bathed them, and put them to bed. They were upstairs as I was downstairs cleaning my carpet and the mess that I had made. It was getting late and I wanted to hear from Vell. I know that he was wrong for sleeping with another woman, but all I thought about was how I could've killed him. I could've lost my freedom and never be able to see my daughters again. I tried not to cry but I couldn't stop. Niecy came back down.

"The girls are sleep and I see that everything is all cleaned up. Are you going to be okay? Do you need me to stay the night with you?" she asked.

"I'm fine and no you don't have to stay, go on home. Thank you for your help, Niecy." I said hugging her.

"Anytime and remember what we talked about. If you need me for anything, just give me a call. I don't care what time it is, call me!" Niecy demanded.

"I will and if you talk to Vell please tell him that I'm sorry." I said giving her a hug before she left out the door. I watched Niecy get in the car and drive off. I went upstairs and went into my daughter's bedroom and they were both sleeping peacefully. I was much too nervous to go to sleep. I went to my bedroom and tried to watch Friday but no matter how funny Smokey was I still couldn't laugh. It was 10p.m. and I thought about calling Vell and if he wasn't going to pick up the phone then I will go to him. The twins were sleeping in bed and wouldn't even know that I was gone. I quickly got dressed and went to get in the car. I sat inside my car for a moment before I pulled off and thought about what I was about to do. I started talking to myself, "I can't leave my daughter's in the house by themselves. If something happen to them, they would lock my black ass up." I marched my silly ass back in the house and got back in the bed. "Fuck it, I'm going to call Loyola and ask for him." I called the hospital and they transferred me to his room. A sleepy Vell answered the hospital phone.

"Hello." Vell said.

"I'm sorry Vell. I'm so sorry." I cried.

"Where are my daughters?" he asked ignoring my apologies.

"They are sleeping in the bed. They're fine." I said.

"You crazy as fuck Aaliyah, but I think that we need a break." Vell said.

"I agree Vell. It's only for the best before someone ends up dead."

"Call me in the morning so that I can speak with my daughters before they leave for school." He said.

"Okay, goodbye." I said ending the call. I looked up above and said thank you to God. I was happy that I didn't kill him. I went to sleep not feeling guilty about what I did.

Meanwhile

Vell laid in the hospital bed stitched up. He had been stabbed multiple times in the torso. Twice in the arm, three times in the chest, and once near his penis. The doctor wanted to keep him overnight for observation. After he ran out of the house to get away from Aaliyah, he drove himself to the hospital. They treated him quickly and pressured him to tell them what happened. The medical professionals were well aware that it was a domestic dispute that occurred due to the areas of the stab wounds. Vell didn't talk or tell them that Aaliyah had stabbed him up. He told him that a complete stranger on the street walked up to him and begun stabbing him. They went along with that story and stopped with the questioning. He didn't want Aaliyah to get into trouble or send the police to his home causing a scene and get into his business. He called Red and told him to come up to Loyola. Once Red made it to the hospital, Vell broke everything down to him and had Red to call Niecy to check on Aaliyah and the twins.

Laying there, he thought about how everything had went down and wished that he could turn back the hands of time. Him and Victoria were having sex and rolled over his phone calling Aaliyah by mistake. He checked the call log in his phone to see that she had been listening to him fucking Victoria for eleven minutes. Knowing that Aaliyah hearing him having sex with another woman had to hurt her. Well was expecting a fight once he made it home. Not once did he ever mean for it to get out of hand the way that it did. He wished he never hurt her, hit her, or have to leave her. Things weren't the same between the two any longer. Aaliyah was not caring, selfish, and was plain boring in bed. It was always her way or no way. Vell dealt with that from day one but it had ran its course. When he first start dealing with Victoria, he felt guilty about it being that she lived next door to them. Aaliyah was always suspicious of their behavior but couldn't ever catch them in the act. He wanted to end it plenty of times but he couldn't because Victoria was the exact opposite of Aaliyah. She was caring, wasn't selfish, and very adventurous in bed. She wasn't messy and didn't talk back. Always remained calm and lady like. The only thing that was keeping Aaliyah and him together were the twins. He loved his daughters, Mia and Mya, and didn't want to see them hurt. A break was the best thing for him to do right now.

When the phone in his room rang, he wasn't surprised that it was Aaliyah calling. He knew that she would call or try to come up there. Victoria begged him to allow her to be by his side but he couldn't risk that. If Aaliyah ever caught them together, she would kill her. Victoria wasn't trying to hear that and still came to be by his side anyway. She was there when she heard Vell talking to Aaliyah on the phone. Pretending like she was sleep on the couch, she became happy when she heard Vell tell her that he needed a break.

Two Days Later

Things felt a little different without Vell being in the house. You know kind of strange, it felt as though he was out of town for a few days. Mia and Mya continued to ask me when was daddy coming back home. I will just tell them soon. Vell called them in the morning and before they went to bed like he promised. I tried to keep myself busy and not think about him. Today was my doctor appointment and I felt so nervous. Although I was still crazy in love with Vell, but I swear if he gave me something I would kill him. I've never been with another man besides him since we both got together. So if anything comes back positive I will kill him then kill myself. I asked Niecy to watch the twins when I went to the doctor. I made it there and the doctor gave me a physical, pap smear, and took some blood. He told me that it could take a day or two for the results to come back and that he would call me once the results were in. I went home and I was a nervous wreck waiting for his call. The only person that I talked to was

Niecy being that she was the only one that knew what was going on. She was very encouraging, real, and calm. I can see why Red was in love with her. Hell she changed that man, to be honest that was the best thing to ever happen to him because Red was hoeish. Once upon a time I didn't like that Vell and Red were friends out of fear that some of Red's bad qualities would rub off on Vell. I realized that people have to make the ultimate decisions to do things and if Vell wanted to cheat he would. You could be the prettiest, smartest, freakiest girl ever but at the end of the day a man will do what he wants to do. I listened to The Way That I Love You by Ashanti over and over again. I could never think in a million years that this could be happening. All the lies, deceit, and games that he pulled on me. I was thinking about who it could be, if it was multiple women, how long it was going on, and what if I do have a disease. All these crazy thoughts ran through my mind.

Sitting in the living room and catching up on the television show Scandal, I was interrupted by my phone ringing. It was the doctor calling, my test results were in and he needed to talk with me. After I hung up, I began crying and shaking, "I swear that nigga better had not gave me shit!" I quickly called Niecy, her phone rang four times before she answered.

"Niecy, my doctor called and asked me to come in today to discuss my test results. I can't do this alone, can you please be there with me?" I asked.

"Sure, I will meet you there. When and where am I going?" she asked.

I gave Niecy the information and two hours later I pulled into the parking lot of my clinic. It took me 15 minutes to get out of the car. Walking slowing into the clinic, I became sick to my stomach and wanted to turn back around. I checked in at the front desk and had a seat waiting for my name to be called. I had on a jogging suit, some gym shoes, and a hat on my head, trying to disguise myself. Hoping not to be identified, hell I hoped that no one would recognize me. A girl that was sitting across from me just stared at me. I caught her looking and rolled my eyes at her. She looked away and picked up the magazine next to her. I checked my phone several times looking at the time. *Niecy, where are you?* I thought to myself. Ten minutes later she walked in and I felt a little better. They called my name and we both walked into the back and had a seat inside my doctor's office. He asked me if it was fine that Niecy was present. I told him yes that it was fine and gave him permission to go ahead.

"Aaliyah Taylor, you came in to be tested on May 15th for an STD Screening. I'm now about to read off your results. First, let me begin with your Pap smear results, those came back normal. You've tested negative for Gonorrhea, Chlamydia, Trichomoniasis, Syphilis, and HIV, but for Herpes you tested positive." He said.

"What are you telling me that I have something that I can't get rid of?" I asked crying.

"Unfortunately, there is no cure for herpes but I can give you medication to reduce your symptoms and make it less likely that you spread the disease to someone else."

"No this is not happening to me!" I cried. Niecy wrapped her arms around me. "Excuse me doctor can you give us a moment?" she asked.

My doctor stepped out leaving the both of us alone. I continued crying, I was hurt, angry, and afraid. Right now, I was so pissed and felt betrayed. "I'm going to fucking kill him!"

"Control yourself Aaliyah, I know that you're upset but people can hear you out there. This is a very personal situation so lower your voice." Niecy said.

"I don't care about being loud! That nigga gave me herpes, I'm going to kill him!" I said storming out of the doctor's office with Niecy running behind me. When I made it to my car and looked back behind me she wasn't there. "Shit! Shit! Shit!" I cursed punching my steering wheel. Niecy tapped on my car window, I rolled my window down and she handed me some paper work from my doctor.

"What is all this?!" I asked with an attitude.

She looked at me with a look that said she wanted to smack the shit out of me. "Information on herpes and your prescription. Aaliyah, I know that you are upset and I can understand your reason why you should be but right now you need to calm the fuck down!" said Niecy.

"Girl fuck keeping calm! When I see Vell's nasty ass, it's on! Thank you for being by my side but right now I don't have time for one of your peep talks, I have to go!"

I sped off leaving Niecy standing in the parking lot. Right now, I didn't need for her to stop me from what I was about to do. Crying and frantically driving around the neighborhood looking for Vell at the spots where he normally frequents wasn't successful. He wasn't nowhere to be found. I was upset but it was cool and I will see his ass real soon. I went to go pick up Mia and Mya. When I made it to their school, I had to get myself together and fix my face. I couldn't let them see me like this. They got inside the car and I snapped back into mommy mode. It was like they kept me calm and relaxed. Besides children need to be children and not have to deal with grown up problems. Once we made it home, I resumed my regular routine, homework, cooking, bathing, and then bedtime. By 8:40 p.m. Vell finally called.

"Let me speak to Mia and Mya." He said.

"Hell nawl, you can't speak to them! I went to the doctor and found out that I have herpes. Your nasty dick trifling ass gave me herpes! Don't you ever in your life come near me or my girls ever fucking again! I hate you!" I cried.

"What the fuck are you talking about?! I didn't give you shit! I don't have no muther fucking herpes!" Vell said angrily.

"You don't know what the fuck you got because you haven't been to see no damn doctor! You out here fucking these hoes raw and me as well. One of them gave you herpes and you gave it to me! I hate you, I hope you die bitch!" I cried into the phone.

"I just got a checkup and I'm telling you that I don't have herpes. Man, I'm gone from this bullshit!" said Vell.

"What you mean bullshit?! You know what fuck you, Vell, and when I see you I'm fucking you up! I hate you, I hate everything about you!"

Vell hung up the phone on me. I can't believe that he lied and said that he just went to the doctor. That's the typical lie that every man uses when you accuse them of giving you a sexually transmitted disease. I sent him a text message of the paperwork showing him my test results just to let him know that it was real. I'm so grateful that he didn't give me HIV with his nasty ass. I bet he out there trying to figure out right know which nasty hoe gave him herpes. There isn't no telling who Vell is sleeping with out there, all I know is that I'm done with him. As far as I'm concerned, he is no longer involved in my life. He can kiss that money in the safe good bye too. I'm using that to take care of me and the twins. I didn't have a job and I wasn't planning on getting one. After all the things that I've did to help him get it, I was damn sure entitled to it. I was his down chick and this how he repays me. That's cool though because I got a trick for easy. If he thinks he's going to get away from this, he has another thing coming. I'm going to make sure that he never passes the shit on to the next female. That's definitely not a threat, that's a muther fucking promise!

Chapter Four

Family Reunion

Ebony

Sitting in my car outside the house that my mother lived in, I contemplated on rather to go and ring her doorbell or pull off never looking back again. I double checked the piece of paper with the address written on it making sure that it was the correct house. The house was nice on the outside. It was a two story brick home with a long brick driveway that led to a three car garage.

"Here goes, its show time." I said to baby Kimora who was sitting in the backseat.

I stepped out and took her out of the car seat proceeding to walk toward the house. I can't believe that I was actually going to do this. I rang the door bell and one minute later a younger girl came to answer the door. She was a younger version of me. She asked me politely, "Hello, how can I help you?"

"I'm looking for Barbara Jones." I said.

The young girl looked back and forth at Kimora and me trying to figure out who we were before she spoke. "Momma!" she yelled never leaving her eyes off of us. I heard someone say yes in the background. "Someone is at the door for you."

A moment later my mother came to the door. She looked at me grabbing her chest. "Oh my God is that you Ebony?" she asked pushing the young girl out of the way hugging me. Kimora began to cry with all the excitement that was going on.

"Yes its me Ebony, momma." I said crying as she hugged me.

"Thank you Jesus! Oh thank you God! Please come inside." My mom invited me and Kimora in. I walked inside and looked around. The house was lovely she had white leather furniture with yellow throw pillows. The yellow and white plush rug was beautiful. It looked like no one has ever sat on the couch before. "Please have a seat, it's fine. Who is this pretty baby that you're holding?" she asked.

"This is my daughter Kimora, she's nine months old." I said rocking her back and forth trying to stop her from crying.

"She is beautiful. This is Emani my daughter, your sister." Emani was looking at me strange. I said hello and she said hey back, dryly. I can tell by her attitude that she was curious about what was going on. Hell, I was too. If Emani was her daughter that meant that she was my sister. Hell, I was confused as well because the last time that my mother tried to reach out to me she never mentioned anything about having another child. I can tell by the look on our mom's face that she had some explaining to do and that it wasn't going to easy. The tension was so thick in the room that you could slice it with a knife. Kimora finally stopped crying and the room was silent. My mother looked at me and Emani back and forth and asked her to sit down on the couch next to me. Emani popped her lips and plopped down on the couch beside me. I could tell that this reunion wasn't going to be a happy one. Kimora was starting to act back up. I went inside her diaper bag and gave her a toy to play with to keep her occupied. I looked back at my mom and she began to speak.

"Ebony, this is your younger sister, Emani. Emani, this is your older sister, Ebony. I know that all this seems crazy right now, but please let me explain to the both of you. Ebony, your father and I were having problems and that's when I met Emani's father and started a new life with him. I ran off and left Chicago because I no longer loved your father and I wanted to be with the man that I loved. I started a new life here in Dallas and several times I've reached out to you Ebony, but you never replied back."

"I'm confused because I still talk to my aunts and didn't no one tell me that you had another child." I said.

"Ebony, they didn't tell you because I asked them not to. I felt that it was my job to break the news to the both of you. Do you mind telling me why you never took the time to reach back to me?" she asked.

"I was angry that you left me and dad breaking up our family. Why did you have to run off with another man? Why didn't you try to work things out between the two of you?" I asked.

My mother looked at Emani, "Emani, can you please excuse the two of us?" she asked her.

"No please stay, she doesn't have to leave after all we all are family right." I said. Emani remained seated. The look on her face showed that she didn't want to leave. "Please continue." I said.

"Ebony look I can't explain why I left but the reason why I didn't fight for our marriage because the love was gone. I never meant to hurt you and I sent for you. Every time I called to speak with you, your father always gave me such a hard time. By the way I am sorry for your loss as well. I went to the funeral back in Chicago. I was hoping to see you there but you weren't." She said.

"You were at my father's funeral? I can't believe that you cared enough to show your respect." I said.

"Just because your father and I separated doesn't mean that I didn't love him unconditionally. May he rest in peace, the past is the past. I would like for us to start all over and be a family. I hope that you find it in your heart to forgive me."

I looked around the house and noticed that it was nice. I smelled money and wondered how much that I could get out of my mom. Hell, I deserved it for all the years that she neglected me. Maybe if she didn't leave me in Chicago I would've grown up to be different. Life would not have been so hard. I decided to play the game and forgive my mother.

"Yes, I forgive you. Even though you weren't around for my life, I would love to have you around for Kimora. Are you ready to be a grandmother?" I jokily asked, easing the tension in the room. My mother laughed but Emani sat right there frowned up not finding anything funny at all. Kimora reached out to her and tried to play with her. I shot Emani a look like, little girl you better play with my daughter before I smack the shit out of you. Emani noticed the look on her face and threw on a fake smile while making baby talk to Kimora. My mother smiled and loved it. "Would you like to hold your granddaughter? I asked.

"I would love too." Kimora went to her grandmother happily.

My mother fell in love with her immediately and asked us to stay over. I accepted and could tell that Emani wasn't too happy about that. I asked for a tour of the house and my mother showed me around. Their home was beautiful with a 10 foot ceiling. On the first floor was the living room and dining room with hardwood floors, a fireplace, and JELD-WEN windows. A white marble dining room set was decorated with yellow vases and a yellow, gray, and black abstract painting hung on the wall. I walked inside the kitchen with its perfect marble floors, granite countertops, stainless steel appliances, and brushed nickel fixtures. She opened the back door and the back had a raised deck with a beautiful big, spacious back yard. We walked upstairs where the four bedrooms were. The master suite was really big with three closets, separate shower, and jetter soaker tub. The Jr. suite had a large closet and private bath. The other two rooms were nice as well. They were living great and in luxury. Nothing like in Chicago. I understand why my mother left daddy, apparently my mother's new husband was paid. While we were in the Jr. suite, I claimed it in my head.

"Where are you and Kimora living?" she asked.

"Not too far from here, about 40 minutes away." I said.

"Oh that's quite a drive. The next time that you two come by feel free to stay and make yourself comfortable. I can tell by the look in your eyes that you love this room." my mother said. She was damn right about that. I was feeling this room but tried to play it off.

"Are you sure? I don't want me or Kimora to be a burden on anyone. From the looks of things around here, there hasn't been a baby around in years."

"You two would never be a burden on us. You are family and we would love to have you and Kimora around. Isn't that right, Emani?" My mother had a big ass smile on her face but Emani wasn't to please. She forced a smile upon her face. "Yes we would love to have you both."

"Great we will love to visit and stay a weekend." I gave my mother a hug. "I'm going to head out and hit the road. It was good connecting back with you." I turned toward Emani, "Nice meeting you sis." I said giving Emani a hug. My mother gave me and Kimora several kisses. I promised her that I would give her a call once I made it home. I waved one more time at them before I pulled off slowly, driving away leaving them standing on the porch. In the meantime I had to get back home and get ready to hit the streets.

Five hours later I was dressed and ready to hit the club. Kimora and her babysitter Miss Stella was sleeping. I didn't even bother to wake them up. I left out the door and made my way to the club. Twenty minutes later I arrived and was ready to party. I walked inside and went straight to the restroom to check myself out. I was perfection baby, my hair was perfect, body was banging in my short mini dress. You couldn't tell me that I wasn't the shit. I applied some lip gloss and popped my lips. After that I exited the restroom and walked through the party. I liked to see who all was in the building. It was still a little early and there wasn't many ballers in the party yet. They usually strolled in after 11p.m. A guy offered to buy me a drink and I accepted it. I ordered some patron and we exchanged numbers. I guess I will add him to list, he was dressed nice and smelled good. I would make sure to call him when I got hungry and wanted to go out to eat. I sipped on my drink and the crowd grew. It was a ruckus and I seen the bouncers dragging two women out of the party. I laughed because it reminded me of the parties back in Chicago when fights broke out. I was chilling and then my crush walked in the party with a few men behind him. You can tell that he was important because they walked him and his entourage straight to VIP. Five minutes later their bottles were coming. I had to get to him tonight without his girl on his side. I went to the restroom to freshen up making sure my breath was on point. Everything was fine and I left out and made myself over toward their section. There were so many women over there and I see that I had some competition. I was cool with that because my candidate was chilling while his buddies was busy talking to the females. I didn't want to seem so thirsty like them so I played it cool and danced to the music alone turning away the few men that tried to dance on me. Out the corner of my eye I could see that I gained his attention. Every time my white mini dress would rise, I will pull it back down and shake my ass harder. I locked eyes with him, bit down on my bottom lip, and winked at him. He nodded his head and I smiled, playing with my hair and dancing to the music. I turned my back on him no longer facing him and continued to dance. I popped hard so that he could see my natural phat ass. He was impressed because one minute later one of his buddies tapped me on the shoulder and invited me to sit with them. I walked over and had a seat right next him. He looked finer than the last time that I've seen him.

He introduced his self, "Hello my name is Tommy, what's your name sexy?" he asked licking his lips.

I thought about giving him my real name but didn't and gave him my middle name instead, "My name is Renee, nice to meet you handsome." I said batting my eyes.

He offered me something to drink, we conversed and exchanged information. He didn't want our conversation to end and neither did I. A few woman watched us and some even rolled their eyes. I didn't give a fuck I was sitting next to the man that I had a crush on and I got his ass. I didn't care that Tia was his girl. Hell, she wasn't a friend of mine, she was only my old dance instructor. I was sipping and laughed and giggled at everything that he said. It was getting late and time to go. I pretended to be tipsy so I held on to his arm leaving out of the club. His car was waiting on him once he stepped outside. He was driving a Benz just one of his cars that I heard that he owned. I wasn't going with him not yet, I didn't want to fuck him so soon. I had plans on staying around and being his side chick not a one night stand. Tommy didn't want me to leave him just yet, he asked if I was straight. "You cool? Where is your car at?" he asked.

"It's parked in the lot. I'm fine I will call you once I make it home. If that is fine with you." I said.

"Yeah you do that sexy. Hit me up and let me know if you cool."

"I will Tommy and you be safe."

"Oh you don't have to worry about me sexy."

I made it to me car and got inside. I was so happy that I met him and plan on sexing him the right way. My sneaky ass had some plans up her sleeves. By the time I get finished with him, I will be getting taken care of and possibly having his baby. I made it home and called Tommy to tell him that I made it home. He answered the phone with his deep voice.

"Hey Tommy, I was just calling you to tell you that I made it in safely. I'm about to get in the shower and after that lay it down." I said.

"Glad to know that you made it home safely sexy. Tell you what if you're free tomorrow lets meet for dinner." He asked.

"I would love that, I will give you a call. I can't wait to see you again. Good night Tommy." I said.

"Bet that's a date, good night sexy."

Oh my god, I can't believe that this was happening. I got him and I wasn't messing this one up like I did with Anthony back in Chicago. I'm aware about Miss Tia being his woman but I heard that they were having problems. I mean after all Tommy did come after me, it wasn't like I threw myself at him. As far I know, he's a single man. I'm not going to ask him about another woman because I don't want to know. If he wants to tell me the truth, then I really don't care. So either way I'm still going to get involved with him and try to sex and finesse him. Hell, Kimora needs a new father and mommy needs a new sponsor.

The next day I woke up and decided to take a jog before Kimora got up. Miss Stella was in the kitchen cooking breakfast. I don't know what it is about old people getting up so damn early. She had cooked grits, eggs, homemade biscuits, and hush puppies. The food smelled amazing, but I had to get my workout on and keep my figure in shape. I walked into the kitchen and said good morning to Miss Stella. I had to get her to watch Kimora again for my date tonight. I didn't plan on needing her for Sunday so I just flat out asked her. I hope that she didn't mind watching Kimora again because I had to see my new boo tonight.

"Miss Stella!" I yelled joking with her, I knew that pissed her off but I loved doing it.

"Girl, what the hell are you yelling for when I'm standing right next to you!?" she said.

"I'm sorry Miss Stella, you know I love playing with you. You're like the grandmother that I never had."

"I see that someone is in a good mood this morning," said Miss Stella.

I went to bathroom and started brushing my teeth, walking back out to talk with Miss Stella. "I met a nice guy last night in the club and I'm just excited." I went back in the bathroom to spit and brush another round leaving Miss Stella in the kitchen running her mouth. I finished up and walked in the kitchen on the tell end of her conversation. She asked his name and was he fine.

"His name is Tommy and yes he is fine. But anyway, can you watch Kimora for another night because he wants to take me out on a date?" I asked, eating a few hush puppies.

Miss Stella smacked my hands. "Yes I will keep her again but you have to pay me extra honey," she said.

"I don't mind paying you extra but let me get ready to jog before Kimora wakes up." I got dressed and grabbed my phone and went to run. I tuned everyone out and played Beyonce as I jogged. A few guys honked their horns trying to flirt, yes baby I was killing shit around here. An hour later I was back at the house and Kimora was sitting in her high chair eating and watching cartoons. Miss Stella was busy cleaning up the mess she had made in the kitchen. I went to shower and after I got out I seen that I had a missed call from Tommy. I was too thirsty to call him back. I needed peace and quiet so I closed my bedroom door. He answered on the first ring, from the sounds of things going on in the background I could tell that he was busy. He answered in such a rush, "Hello what's up sexy?"

"Hey Mr. just returning your call back." I said.

"I was just giving you a call and making sure we are still on for tonight." He said.

"Yes we are I can't wait to see you." I said.

"Cool you pick out the restaurant, where ever you want to go it's cool with me."

"Great. I will do that and give you a call back with my decision." I said drying my body off with my bath towel. He agreed and ended the call. I wanted to send him a nude picture of my body so bad but it was too soon for that. I got myself together and for the rest of the day I was going to spend it with my precious Kimora until it was time for my date.

~~~~~~

I arrived at the restaurant ten minutes early. I called my mother and asked her what would be a romantic place to have dinner and she suggested SER Steak + Spirits. I walked inside and the hostess greeted me. "Hello welcome to SER Steak + Spirits, how many people will be joining you?"

"Hello. I have reservations for two under the name Renee." I said.

She looked down on the paper to find my name and grabbed two menus and asked me to follow her. Walking behind her, I could feel all the eyes that were watching me. I couldn't blame them. Hell, I looked good wearing my low cut, red bandage dress that revealed my ample breasts. My nude color red bottoms tapped on the marble floors. We made it to the table, I took a seat and waited for Tommy to arrive. The view from the 27th floor was breathtaking, you could see all of Dallas. Five minutes later Tommy arrived looking good wearing a white collar shirt with a nice pair of jeans and some white air force ones. He had a seat with his glistening diamonds in his ears. I was so nervous when he spoke to me that it took me a moment to speak back. When he called me Renee I'd almost forgot that I didn't tell him my real name, Ebony. My dumb ass almost fucked that up but I snapped back. We ordered our food and got better acquainted with one another. I listened to Tommy talk and thought to myself how I've never dated a guy like him before ever. The date was going fine, the atmosphere was perfect. The piano player serenaded everyone with his sounds. The duck that the chef prepared was delicious. Tommy asked me several questions about my life. I lied about everything from my name, where I'm from, and that I didn't have a daughter. He didn't need to know the truth because I was about to play his ass. I had to remind myself several times to cut my feelings off and focus back on the money. Tommy kept saying that I looked familiar and that he seen me from somewhere before. It was my turn to ask the questions and I asked him if he had a woman and of course he lied and said that he was single. By that time I had two glasses of wine and was starting to feel myself. My hoe tendencies were starting to kick in. I was thinking about all the nasty things that I wanted to do with him. He picked up on my vibe and begin to caress my thighs under the table. I smiled opening my legs up a little wider.

"Looking for something?" I asked, flirting with him.

"Yes, I am sexy, can you help me find it?" he asked as his hands creped up my thighs.

I smacked his hands away laughing, "Cut it out before you start something that you can't finish." We both laughed, he asked if I was ready to go and I replied, "Yes but I don't want this date to end."

He licked his lips, "It doesn't have to sexy if you don't want it too." I looked into his eyes and smiled.

One Hour Later

"I'm so embarrassed, I usually don't sleep with men on the first date. I feel so ashamed and easy." I said lying knowing damn well I was a certified whore.

"It's cool sexy. I'm feeling your sexy ass. No need to be ashamed because I don't look at you any different. Besides, not trying to sound cocky but you were going to give me the pussy anyway." He laughed.

"Sounds pretty cocky to me, you just knew that you were going to get fucked tonight." I hit him playfully while sitting up in the bed. "I hope that we could do this more often because I'm feeling you too."

"As long as you don't start to acting crazy, you can be around for a very long time."

"Me acting crazy, never that. I'm a pretty laid back chick. You don't have to worry about any such things. I'm such a lady." I smiled and went back to sucking his dick. Tommy continued to talk. I heard him mention that he was going out of town for a week. I didn't like to hear that, but I had no choice but to accept it. We fucked one more time before I left.

Chapter Five

Tia

I'm so excited about my trip and my birthday. This was the very first time that Tommy and I have ever been outside the country and had to use our passports. I made sure that I packed as many swimsuits as possible. Tommy walked in and seen me packing my suitcases. "Damn baby, what you taking the whole closet with you?" he joked.

"I have one suitcase filled with clothes, one with shoes, and another one filled with my swimsuits and other personal items." I said.

He laughed, "We only going for a week, baby. You packing like we going to be gone for a month."

I sat down on my suitcase filled with clothes pushing it together while zipping it up. He laughed and grabbed the bags rolling and carrying them to the car. I hugged my man from behind and rubbed his muscular arms. "I love all of you, you're so damn strong."

He turned around facing me and gave me a kiss. "I love you too but don't try to butter me up."

I checked everything in the house making sure that nothing was left on and that all the windows and doors were locked before we left. My sister Traci agreed to check on my place daily while we were out of town. We left and drove to the airport, I suggested that we hire a driver. Tommy didn't want do to that so we used airport parking and left his Cadillac truck parked there until we came back. We boarded our flight. I'm not going to lie I was scared to take this flight. I popped me a pill to ease me. I prayed for a safe flight and was up, up, up, and away. Fours later we made it to Jamaica I was rested and ready to turn up for my birthday. I called my mom and sisters informing them all that we made it safely.

"Montego Bay we have arrived." I happily said. We were staying at Round Hill Hotel and Villas in an ocean view suite. It was an adult only hotel with plenty to do. Tommy and I didn't waste any time unpacking and unwinding. I threw on my hot red monokini with some red flip flops. Tommy was wearing red swim trunks to match. We grabbed our towels and hopped on a spacious catamaran that took us across the sea. There was a crowd of people partying, the dee jay had everyone dancing as he blasted hip hop music. Tommy and I were enjoying ourselves. We went straight to the bar and ordered drink after drink. Tommy tried to talk me into going snorkeling but that wasn't going to happen. I told him he wasn't allowed to do it either, shit that's too deep to be going down to the bottom of the sea. Once we landed on the beach, I ran and jumped in the beautiful water. Tommy joined me and dunked me several times. I was soaking wet he carried me away off the ocean.

"You're so beautiful." He said as he looked into my eyes. It was something different about him at the moment that I didn't want to ever go away. I was speechless and kissed him instead. We continued to play in the water. I was doing handstands and splits. Tommy took several pictures of me on the beach as well as partying on the catamaran. I wasn't ready to turn down once we made it back to Montego Bay. It was still early so we rented water scooters. Tommy and I raced on Doctor's Cave beach. One hour later hunger was starting to kick and we worked up an appetite. We went back to our room to prepare for dinner. Tommy told me that he had a surprise for me. I wonder what the surprise was as I got ready, you better believe that I asked him several times but he wouldn't tell me. I slipped on my white, one shoulder maxi dress with silver accessories and sandals. Tommy had on a white linen suit, we both complimented one another.

"You looking good as hell in that dress, baby." Tommy rubbed his hands together and licked his lips as he kept his eyes on my ass.

"Thank you Mr., you're looking handsome as well."

"Are you ready for your surprise?" he asked.

"Yes I am!" I anxiously said.

"You have to let me blindfold you." Tommy covered my eyes with a piece of cloth and led me on the beach. I could feel the sand between my toes anticipating what I was about to see. "Are you ready? I'm about to take off the blindfold."

My heart was racing, "Yes I'm ready." Tommy removed the blindfold, I couldn't believe what I was seeing right before my eyes. I was shocked, surprised, and pleased.

"Happy birthday baby, I love you!" he said. I was speechless, I couldn't believe that he did all of this for me. It was a table set up with food, candle light, and yellow roses were scattered everywhere. A waiter was present as well standing by waiting to serve us and a band of men played Caribbean music. It was so romantic that I started to cry.

"This is so beautiful, Tommy I love you!" He wiped my tears away, grabbed my hand, and pulled out my chair to sit. We both sat down and the waiter announced that we were having steak, lobster, shrimp, and our sides were broccoli au gratin and asparagus. He poured champagne in our glasses.

"All of this for me, this is so wonderful. You really surprised me, baby. This is the best birthday gift ever!" I said.

"Anything for you, baby. You know I had to go all out for you. You mean the world to me, Tia. I love you so much." Tommy kissed my right hand and got down on one knee.

"Oh my God! Oh my God! This is not really happening!" I said holding my hands over my mouth in excitement.

"Tia from the moment I met you I knew that you were the one. We've had our ups and downs, highs and lows, but through it all you stuck by my side. I love you for that, you mean the world to me and I want to spend the rest of my life with you. Tia will you do me the honor of becoming my wife, will you marry me?"

"Yes! Yes! Yes! I will marry you Tommy. Give me my ring!" I said happily.

Tommy slid the ring on my finger. I looked at it and jumped into his arms. "I love you so much Tommy always and forever."

"I love you too forever, baby." Tommy said.

The remaining of my birthday trip was nothing but fun, fun, fun! Unfortunately, it has come to an end and is now over with. We packed our things and was on our way to the airport. I called my family telling them that we were on our way home. We boarded the plane and Tommy and I slept the entire flight on our way. We were dead beat tired from all the fun that we had. As soon as we made it back home, Tommy perked up and got a burst of energy out of know where. It was still pretty early in the afternoon and it felt good to be back home. I, on the other hand, was still a little restless. The moment I walked through my front door the only thing I wanted to do was relax and share the news of my engagement. I couldn't wait to show off my five carat, princess cut diamond ring to my mother and sisters. It stood out on my finger, I was blinging baby. I unpacked a few on my things while Tommy talked on the phone. Twenty minutes later he was out the door to handle business. Not wasting any time getting back to the money, I made a few phone calls checking on my business. I was excited to start filming my 'Tia Teach Me How Too Strip' videos. This was a big and major step in my life. After I was done taking care of business, it was time to kick back, relax, and unwind. My cell phone disturbed me and Ciara picture popped up on my phone screen as a FaceTime call.

"What's up Ci Ci." I said smiling.

"Hey Tee Tee luv. How was Jamaica? What did you get for your birthday? Girl don't leave anything out," she said sipping on a glass of wine.

"Jamaica was awesome!" I displayed my finger showing off my wedding ring.

"No are you serious! Congratulations Tia, girl you is blinging. How did he ask you?"

"Ciara, he tricked me." I giggled. "Tommy blindfolded and led me to the beach where he surprised me with a candlelight dinner on the beach. Girl, he had a band playing and everything. It took me moment to take all that in. Just when I thought that was the surprise, he got down on bended knee asking for my hand in marriage."

"Damn that was very romantic. I'm so happy for you friend or should I say family." Ciara said smiling and sipping.

"Thank you, I still can't believe it. It's like a dream come true to me. You have no idea how much I love Tommy. We've been through a lot, one minute we're fighting and the next minute we're laughing. But during both times, we never stop loving one another. It's like we understand one another, you know what I'm saying."

"If anyone understands, you know that I'm that girl. Being that Smooth and I have had our battles with cheating, getting women pregnant, and me going upside a broad head. Throughout it all I still love that man. Sometimes we can't help who we love." Ciara said with a sad look upon her face.

"You're right about that, but enough about me. What's going on with you? I see you sipping on your glass of wine. If I do recall, I don't think that you are supposed to be drinking. Is everything cool in Chicago?" I asked being concerned.

"Yes everything is fine. Can a girl enjoy one glass of wine?" Ciara laughed but I didn't find it funny.

"Where is everybody at Ciara?"

"The children are in their rooms and ain't no telling where Smooth is girl. Wait, hold on I have another call." Ciara looked at who was calling she frowned and continued talking. I could tell by the look on her face that she didn't want to be bothered with whomever was calling her. "I'm not answering so anyway what were we talking about again?" Ciara said.

"Who was that Ciara?"

"That was Kanye. He keeps on calling and texting me every hour saying that he wants to talk."

"That explains why you're drinking. So what are you going to do about him?" I asked.

"I don't know a part of me misses him and really wants to hear what he has to say. Another part of me wants to forget that I've never met him and cut him off completely. My feelings are all over the place right now. What should I do Tia?"

"I think that you should talk to him at least hear what he has to say. There isn't nothing wrong with that."

"You right about that." She paused and looked back as if she seen someone. "Wait a second girl, I think Smooth is home. Yes he's here, Tia we have to continue this conversation tomorrow. Congratulations to you and Tommy. I love you," she said guzzling down the last of her wine.

"Thanks and you better call me back. Tell everyone I said hello and I love you too. Talk to you later, Ciara."

After the phone call was over she got me to thinking about my man. I hit Tommy up to check on him. He answered the phone with his loud music blasting in the background. I hated when he had the music up really loud because I couldn't hear what was going on in the background.

"Turn down that damn music! What are you doing?" I said.

"I'm chilling, what's up bae? Everything good? You cool?" Tommy asked he still had he music up loud as hell.

"I'm cool just checking on you. I haven't heard from you since you left out the door. How much longer will you be out? Before you come home can you stop off to pick me up something to eat?" I asked.

"I got you bae and please don't start questioning me. I will be home in a minute." He said.

"You be safe out there and I love you Tommy."

"I love you too, be there shortly." **Click.**

Some things will never change when it comes to him and I. He lucky that I'm too damn exhausted to get up, throw on some clothes, and ride around looking for his ass. I was being a good girl and not a crazy one, besides I had this nice ring on my finger and too much other things going on in my life at the moment. No I don't trust his ass as far as I can throw him and if Tommy wants to fuck things up that's on him. I will leave his ass high and dry and take everything that nigga had. He would have to start all over. I'm not playing, he could try me if he want to. Let me calm down and stop jumping to conclusions and shit. I'm feeling some type of way maybe because of Ciara's situation. I can't really compare our relationship with my friend's relationship because Tommy's past and mine seem to come into play from time to time. I really need to work on leaving the past behind.

Tommy

"Oh shit! Get all that dick in your mouth sexy!" I sat back enjoying the head job that Renee was giving me. She was sucking the life out of my dick. No gag reflex, my dick went down her throat like it belonged there. Her tongue skills were remarkable. I rode around the city as she sucked and slurped on my dick. She was a keeper and what I liked about her was she didn't stop sucking on my dick when Tia called me. I am glad that I hit her on the line after I finished taking care of all my business. She said she missed me once she got in the car. *How much did she miss me?* I wondered. That's when she pulled my dick out and showed me. Damn and she wasn't lying about missing me. Five minutes later I busted down her throat. Renee sat up and looked at me smiling, "Do you believe that I miss you?" she asked. Her eyes expressed that she did but what I couldn't understand is how could you miss something that you never had. I still haven't spent much time wirh her to be missing out on anything. Right now, she was cool and shit was flowing fine. I just hope that she doesn't switch up on me.

I went on to tell her what she wanted to hear. "Hell yeah, I believe you sexy. You didn't waste any time proving it."

"Did you enjoy it? You know that I don't usually do things like this. I hope that you don't look at me different now." Renee said with lying lips. I don't know who she thought she was fooling but it sure in the fuck wasn't me.

I ignored that comment and changed the subject. "What all did you do while I was away?"

"I've been busy looking for a job."

"Did you have any luck and what line of work are you in?" He asked.

"Unfortunately, I didn't have any luck. I'm looking for something that pays the bills. Anything that has a steady cash flow. I'm so desperate that I even thought about giving stripping a try."

"Don't get discouraged I'm pretty sure that something would open up soon for you. Stripping ain't for you sexy. Other than that are you straight? Is there anything that I could do to help?"

"Well, since you asked I do need a few bucks to buy me some food. My fridge is a little bare."

"I tell you what, I will hit you in the morning to run you to the grocery store. If you hungry now, we could grab you something to eat right now."

"That's cool with me because I'm starving."

We rode to the restaurant and I bought her and wifey something to eat. Tia had called me back several times but I didn't answer the phone in front of Renee. I dropped her ass off and hurried home. When I walked inside, I could hear Mary J. Blige playing in the bedroom. Tia was sipping wine wearing a black lace panty and bra set. Her back was turned away from the door. She didn't hear me come in, I sacred her causing her to grab her gun that she had sitting on the nightstand. I put my hands up in the air, "Cool baby, it's just me!" I said quickly.

"Damn Tommy, why in the hell are you creeping in on me like that and where the hell have you been? I've been calling your phone for the last hour!" she said while turning off the music with the remote control.

"Baby, I was out handling business and plus I had to stop off and grab you something to eat." All the food was on the floor. I bent down to clean up the mess.

"Fuck that food Tommy if I call your phone again and you don't answer there's going to be some problems around this bitch!" Tia followed me in the bathroom talking crazy. I undressed and jumped in the shower. She was still running her mouth, luckily I couldn't hear her because of the running water. When I got out, she was laying down frowned up. I knew that I had to change that into a smile because I didn't want her to go to bed upset with me.

"Why are you frowned up, baby?" I tried to give her a hug but she pushed me off of her.

"Get the hell off of me Tommy! You got some nerve asking me some dumb shit like that."

"Tia stop playing with me!" I grabbed her pinning her down and smothered her with kisses. Her tiny punches couldn't stop me so Tia resist from fighting. I kissed and suck on her earlobe and neck. I went a little lower stopping at her belly button. She giggled every time I licked her navel. Working my way down and separating her thick thighs, I kissed the insides of each. My tongue flicked on her clit. "Oh Tommy!" Tia moaned. I buried my head into her juicy pussy, she arched her back and pushed my head in deeper. "Yes Tommy! Ohhhh yes!" she said I as I rapidly flicked my tongue on her clit. I opened up her lips and sucked hard on her clit. Her body twist and turned in ecstasy. I slurped on her pussy until she exploded in my mouth. "Ahhh, lick it up baby!" she said.

The next day I didn't rush outside instead I spent the morning with Tia. She was my baby and I felt kind of guilty about last night. Besides I don't want to fall out with my baby and cause any problems in our relationship. When I asked her to marry me, I was serious about everything, being my wife and having my kids. Yeah I know that I have a few chicks on the side but don't none of them compare to my baby, Tia. She's my queen and one day she will have my little princess or prince, I'm hoping for both. We spent our morning making love. After that we had breakfast and discussed her new major project. I was happy that my woman's career was going great. I admired how she worked her ass off and turned her passion into something bigger. That's what I loved about her the most, she was dedicated and determined to make it despite all the harsh criticism she faced when everyone found out about her stripping. We both reminisced the moment when she came to me about teaching pole dancing. I honestly doubted that it would take off. She proved me wrong making a good profit her first year. She started off from teaching only day classes to teaching afternoon, evening, and weekend classes. Spent all her time building her company and threw me back the money that I gave her to start with. Tia was definitely a winner, fighter, rider, and go getter. After breakfast she was ready to hang out with her family. I remember I had promise Renee that I would buy her some food. I didn't want to spin off sexy and stop receiving that good head. Hey, I feel like every man is entitled to have a girl on the side. I think that she was going to be that one as long as she knew how to act. I pulled up in front of Tia's mom house.

"Tell momma I said hello, baby." I said to Tia as she got out of the car.

"You park, come inside and tell her yourself." Tia said.

I ran inside real quick to say hello to the family. Tia's mother and sisters were all there. This was my first time seeing them all together in a while. They were all excited about our engagement. Her mother was in the kitchen cooking a big meal and had the house smelling good. I gave her a hug and she questioned me on my whereabouts. I laughed it off and told her that I had to make money to take care of her daughter. Tia stood by laughing, I gave her a kiss and told her that I will be back in two hours. I left and once I returned back to my car I noticed that Renee had called on my second phone that I had. I called her back and told her to meet me at a grocery store across town. Thirty minutes later I pulled up in the parking lot and parked my car next to hers. I know that I could've just gave her the money but I wanted to make sure that she actually spent it on food. The last time I gave a female four hundred dollars she spent it on hair weave instead of getting Christmas toys for her children. Renee looked nice in her jogging suit and gym shoes. She gave me a hug and I grabbed her big ass and squeezed it. We walked inside the food market and she grabbed a shopping cart.

"Get what whatever you need sexy." I said.

"You sure you telling me that I could buy whatever I want?" Renee asked.

"Yeah, it's cool sexy."

Renee went down every aisle throwing everything in the cart from fruit, meat, to junk food. As we shopped I was trying to recall where the hell I knew her from. It was starting to bother me because I usually remember a person. I guess the way I was looking at her made Renee question me. "Why are you looking at me like that?" she giggled.

"You look so familiar, I'm trying to recall where I've seen your face from before." I said.

"Maybe I just look like someone you may know. You know what they say; we all have a twin out here somewhere floating around."

Forty minutes later we checked out. I paid for $400 dollars' worth of groceries. That should cover her for at least two months since it was only her who had to eat. We walked back to her car and I placed the food inside her trunk.

"Thank you, Tommy. No man has ever did this for me before. I really appreciate it because you didn't have to do this." Renee said. We were hugged up against her car as she stood on her tiptoes and gave me a kiss on the cheek.

"No problem sexy." I said while looking at watch. "Let me get on my way. You good?" I asked.

"Yes I am. I have more than enough food." She said.

"Cool hit me up when you make it home to let me know that you're straight."

I jumped in my car and sped off. I had to make one more stop before heading back to Tia's mother house. I spent more time than expected in the grocery store. I know Tia was wondering when I was going to make it back. Her mother wasn't even finished cooking the food when I dropped her off. Which was good because by the time that I make it back the food should be hot and ready. While making a few stops, I called my cuz Smooth to holler at him for a minute.

"What's up Cuz? What's going on with cha in the Chi?" I asked.

"Man you know me, just trying to stay sucker free. What's this I hear about you proposing to Tia in Jamaica?" he laughed.

"Yeah man I went on and popped the question. It's time to make it official." I said.

"That's what happening, Congratulations Cuz! What's going on down there on the money side, you good?"

"Everything is grand, you know how I do it. I have to holler at my partner today about what we talked about. We in good hands everything is going to come thru." I assured him.

"Ok cool that's what I wanna hear. Cuz check it out, I will hit you back later Ciara just walked in."

"Cool tell Ciara I said what's up. I'll holler at cha later Smooth."

Ciara said hello back and asked about Tia. Speaking of Tia, I had to be making my way back to her soon before she kills me. As soon as I ended the call with Smooth, Tia was ringing on the other phone. When I answered all I heard was her mother yelling in the background, "Tell him to get his ass back here!" I laughed and told wifey that I was on my way. It didn't take long for me to make it back to my mother in law house. When I pulled up, Tia walked out on the porch to meet me. She seemed somewhat upset. I prepared myself and was ready to hear her mouth. When I reached the porch, I wrapped my arms around her. Tia had a slight frown on her face, but I managed to get a couple of kisses from her. We went inside and I made myself comfortable while her mother and sisters chewed me up for having them waiting. Tia went to go make a plate as I continued to talk with everyone. When she brought the plate, she still didn't seem like herself but joined in on the conversation. I think her mother felt that something was wrong but didn't want to ask. Two hours later we prepared to go home. The ride on the way home was quiet, every time I asked Tia something she would reply back dryly with one word. I knew that meant she was pissed about something. Once we got inside I've had enough of her silent treatment.

"Tia, what's wrong baby? If it's about me being late I apologize and it won't happen again." I said. Tia went inside our bedroom closet and came back out undressed wearing only her white bra, boy shorts, and pumps. She removed her pumps and threw them both at me. "Ouch!" I didn't get out of the way fast enough. "Why the fuck you throwing shoes at me, baby? Chill out with all that crazy shit Tia!"

"Don't tell me to chill out! Tommy who the fuck were you with at the grocery store earlier today?!" She asked getting all up in my face.

"What?! I wasn't at no damn grocery store with nobody!" I lied and said.

"Tommy, I received a phone call today from a reliable source telling me that they seen you grocery shopping with some bitch! I just know that they were lying until she sent me a picture of you walking right beside the bitch with your hand on her ass as she pushed the shopping cart." Tia pulled out her IPhone and showed me the picture. It was a shot of me just as she described. The person who snapped the picture of us took one of our backs. Tia was steaming and close enough in my face that I could smell her minty breath. She pointed her index finger into the side of my head several times.

"Tommy, how can you explain that?! Who is this bitch?! Where did she come from?! How long have you been fucking with this one?! This one has to be your girlfriend, you both grocery shopping and shit like a happy couple! You always managed to help out these needy hoes!" Tia said.

I grabbed her right hand and she smacked me with her left hand quickly. "Smack!" I threw her on the bed. "Chill out Tia before I fuck you up! I don't know what the hell you talking. I ain't going to tell you but one time to keep your hands to yourself."

"Tommy, you keep on playing with me and my emotions thinking that our relationship is a game. I'm sitting at my mother's house celebrating or engagement, which I felt and thought was real. I realize that you asking me to marry you means nothing to you at all." Tia took the five carat ring off and threw that at me. "Fuck you and this ring! It doesn't mean anything to you and I'm not going to be wearing a ring looking like a damn fool."

"Tia, you gonna believe what the hell they tell you. That's not me on that picture, I wasn't at no damn grocery store!" I said.

"So you think that I'm fool? Look at you and look at the picture." She pushed the phone in my face. "From head to toe, that's you! Your dreads, your shirt, your jeans, your hand with displays your Rolex on your wrist with your hand on her ass, and your Gucci sneakers." **Pow! Pow!** Tia punched me twice in my face.

This time I pinned her ass down on the bed. "Didn't I tell you to keep your fucking hands to yourself? You must want to get fucked up, Tia!"

"I wish you would put your got damn hands on me. You best bet is that you get your shit and get the hell out of here because if you don't I might fuck around and kill you." She said out of breath. I wouldn't let her hands go so she started kicking me in the stomach. "Let me go and get the fuck on! I don't care where you go but you got to get the hell up out of here!" Tia yelled!

Chapter Six

Ciara

Today was a busy day at the boutique and I was tired as hell. I was a little pissed off at Smooth for asking me to meet him downtown. When I asked why he needed me to meet him downtown, he told me that it was a business matter and that I needed to be present. He also made sure that his mother went to go pick up the children from school as well. I fought my way through rush hour traffic and made it on time. I looked at the address and drove into the underground parking lot. I called Smooth and he was there waiting on me. When I stepped off the elevator, I walked down the hall to Suite 1750. I entered and a young lady was sitting behind a desk.

"Hello, how can I help you?" She politely asked.

"Hi, I'm here to meet my husband Eric." I said. The young lady picked up the phone and told someone that I was here.

"Mrs. Jackson your husband is waiting for you. Please follow me," she said.

I followed her down the hall and into a room that said, Emily Wilson PhD. I walked inside the room and Smooth was sitting down talking with a woman that looked familiar.

"Hey baby, I'm so happy that you made it." Smooth said standing up giving me a kiss and a hug. I played along with it but I was going to let his ass have it once we made it home.

The woman spoke, "Ciara Robinson, is that you?"
She asked. I looked at her really hard and I couldn't believe
that it was Mrs. Wilson, my counselor from the group
home. "Mrs. Wilson, oh my god, I haven't seen you in such
a very long time. I'm now Ciara Jackson," I said. We both
hugged one another.

"Ciara, you have grown up to become a beautiful
young lady. I had the chance to meet and talk with your
husband, by the way who's very respectable. Why don't we
all have a seat and begin with our session," said Mrs.
Wilson.

"Wait hold up, what do you mean session? Smooth
what is going on?" I asked looking at him like he was crazy
with my hands on my hips.

Mrs. Wilson looked over at Smooth. "I'm sorry I
thought that you were aware of why you were here."
Smooth spoke up and ended all this confusion.

"Ciara, I went ahead to seek out help regarding your
drinking and came across Mrs. Wilson." Smooth said.

"So you just up and do things behind my back
without my knowledge?" I shook my head as I paced back
and forth.

"I gave you plenty of times to seek counseling but
you're in denial about your drinking problem." Smooth
said.

"You know what Smooth I don't have a drinking
problem. As a matter of fact, I haven't had a drink in a
month." I lied and said. Smooth gave me a look that said,
please stop lying. I was about to check his ass but Mrs.
Wilson intercepted.

"Ciara, please have a seat so that we all could discuss the matter. I know that you are upset about being misled here by Eric, but Ciara he felt that he had to make the appropriate steps in order to get you help." She said.

"Okay. I will sit down only because you asked me to but trust and believe I'm not feeling any of this." I said while sitting down. I moved my chair as far away from Smooth as possible. He looked at me like I was crazy and moved his chair closer to mine. I looked at him and exhaled as I thought about the things that made me happy and ignored his ass. Smooth tried to hold my hand but I snatched it away from him. Mrs. Wilson watched the both of us scribbling shit down and started with our session.

"Now that we are all aware of what brought us all here today we can begin. Usually, I prefer to have my clients start off first by sharing what is bothering them. With that being said, Ciara feel free to go first." She said.

"I don't have a drinking problem. No offense to you Mrs. Wilson but I don't want to be here." I said.

"None taken Ciara. Eric would you like to begin?" Mrs. Wilson asked.

"Ciara does have a drinking problem. I have found several wine and liquor bottles hidden in various areas in our home. It has gotten so bad that I can't bring alcohol into my home. Just the other day I came home and she had been drinking because I could smell it on her breath. I have smelled alcohol on her several times but I don't question her because I don't want to start a fight." Smooth said.

"Ciara does any of this behavior sound familiar to you?" Mrs. Wilson asked. I just sat there quietly and ignored the both of them.

Smooth held my hand. "Ciara, I love you and I'm trying to help you." He said looking into my eyes. At that moment I felt like he had lit a spark in me and I exploded.

"Love me? You don't love anyone but yourself! As a matter of fact, he's the reason why I started drinking in the first place. His lies, cheating ways, and unnecessary drama that he has put me through has drained me. Having a daughter with a psycho bitch that made our lives a living hell. From day one she provoked and picked on me. She mailed a letter and pictures to my home too, even showing up at my wedding trying to kill me. All because of you! Yes I started drinking but it's not a problem. After everything that you have put me through you lucky that I haven't lost it and killed your ass!" I said.

"Ciara, you act as though I was aware of my daughter. I had a one-time fling with Rochelle before I met you." Smooth said.

"It's not about you and Rochelle one time fling. It's about how you kept Erica a secret from me. Why did I have to find out through her? If you love me you would've been upfront about everything. You were busy playing house and taking family portraits with her while I was at home pregnant and alone. How do you think I felt when I found out about you having another child? I felt stupid and I was thinking that I was having your first born. It hurt me Smooth. It still hurts till this day!" I cried.

Mrs. Wilson grabbed the box of tissue and handed me a few pieces to wipe my face. It felt good getting all of that off of my chest. Smooth wrapped his arms around me and held me in his arms as I cried. "Don't cry baby, I never meant to hurt you." He lifted my head up and looked into my eyes. He was crying, "I love you Ciara." He kissed me softly, but I turned my head away.

"Would you two like to continue with session? I see right now things have gotten very emotional in here," said Mrs. Wilson.

"I don't really want to continue. I just would like to get out of here and go home." I sniffed and said wiping my face with the tissue.

Smooth looked deep into my eyes. "Ciara, I know that all my actions in the past has caused a lot of confusion in our life but I never intended to hurt you. I care so much about you and my family. I love and appreciate you. You are a strong woman and a great mother. I'm so lucky to have you in my life. Please don't you ever think for a second that I don't care about you or that I don't love you. I will die and kill for you. I love you Ciara with all my heart. You're my Blackbone and backbone."

He kissed me on my forehead. I thought about everything that he just said and suddenly I felt guilty about seeing Kanye in the past. Maybe Smooth does care about me, after all, if he didn't he wouldn't have set all this up. I was lost without words at the moment and was pretty much ready to go home and get some rest. Honestly, I wanted a drink badly now, a sweet glass of Moscato would be great right about now. I gathered my things and prepared to go. "Mrs. Wilson thank you and I must admit that it felt good to talk about the way that I feel inside. I would love to see you again." I said.

"Great let's set up another appointment. Eric do you mind if I speak with Ciara privately?" she asked.

"No problem I will be in front waiting on you." He said kissing me once again before leaving out the room. "Have a seat Ciara." Mrs. Wilson said. I sat down and felt like I was back meeting her again in the group home. Mrs. Wilson could tell that I was timid so she held my hand.

"Ciara, first off, I would like to say that what you did today was great. The first part getting help for your addiction is admitting that you have a problem. Second have you touched basics with your mother? I do recall that you hated her because of everything that she did."

"Yes I reunited back with my mother and we have grown to love one another. I have forgiven her and left that in the past. My mother is doing great now she doesn't drink anymore and has turned her life to God." I said.

"That's great do you mind if she attends the next session with you instead of your husband?" Mrs. Wilson asked.

"I don't mind at all. I will ask her today but I'm more than sure that it wouldn't be a problem." I said.

"Great. I will see you next week."

I gave Mrs. Wilson a hug and met Smooth in the lobby where he was waiting for me. I set up an appointment for next. Luckily, I remembered my mother's work schedule by heart. So I scheduled it on one of her days off. Smooth and I both left and he walked me to my car. I asked him if he wanted me to pick the children up from his mother's house but he told me and to go straight on home. I did what he asked me too and was happy that the ride home didn't take too long. When I got inside, I ran my bath water and soaked in the Jacuzzi. I was craving a glass of wine so bad but I couldn't do because I will start off with one glass and ten minutes later the bottle would be empty. Instead, I soaked all my pain away and drifted off to sleep and starting dreaming about Kanye. He was here in my home massaging my body as I laid naked in bed. His big hands rubbed and caressed my back. Kanye worked his way down to my ass and gently rubbed it. Separating my thighs, he worked his between my legs. "Ohhhh!" I moaned as he stroked my kitty.

"Mommy! Mommy!" The children came running inside my bedroom.

"Damn." I mumbled under my breath. "I'm in the bathroom!" I yelled as I got out and wrapped a towel around my body. Erica and Eric Jr. ran inside and gave me a big hug. I kissed and hugged the both of them. They told me everything that did over their grandmother house and how they played with the baby.

"Mommy, grandma baked us some cookies and let me hold the baby." Erica said.

"That's so cool. Whose baby are you talking about?" I asked her as Smooth walked into the room the joined us.

"My mother was watching one of my little cousin baby. Erica and Jr. you two go on ahead and get ready for bed" Smooth said.

"Okay daddy." They both kissed me good night and ran in their rooms to get ready for bed. I grabbed the baby oil and started oiling up my body. Smooth unbuttoned his shirt but was stopped by the cries of Jr.

"Go and check on your son." I laughed and said. By the look on Smooth's face he didn't want to but had to. I continued oiling my body and after I was done I put on my black satin rug. I made myself comfortable and laid down in bed. Smooth came back in and went to take a shower. When he got out he sat on the bed next me and removed my robe and rubbed my body down. His hands felt so good rubbing up and down my body. I was hot and ready and couldn't resist it any longer so I turned around and pulled him aggressively to me. We tongued kissed and Smooth slipped inside my wet pussy. He threw my legs over his shoulders and pumped in and out of me. I fantasized about Kanye as Smooth fucked the shit out of me.

"Ohhh! Please don't stop!" I moaned.

"Yesss, this pussy is good! This pussy is so damn good and wet!" Smooth said.

"Fuck me harder!" I demanded. Smooth sped up hitting my pussy harder. I was on the verge of exploding.

"Whose pussy is this?!" he asked.

"Your pussy!" I moaned as I continued to fantasize about Kanye.

"Whose pussy is this?!"

"K a n y e, Smooth! Ohhhh Smooth!" I screamed. Smooth sweaty body collapsed on top of me. He was enjoying his nut that he just busted that he didn't even noticed that I had almost called him ans screamed out another man's name during sex. I slid from under him and walked in our bathroom, grabbed a wash cloth and wet it. I quickly washed my face and stared at myself in the mirror.

"Ciara, you got to get it together girl." I said to myself splashing water on my face. I went to lay next to Smooth who was snoring and knocked out. A girl still had it I see just like the first time. If things keep going on this way maybe we could get back to being one big happy family again. I would really love to have it that way again and I would do whatever it takes to keep us together. Today I learned that holding things inside wasn't healthy for you. It was time for me to start back loving Ciara, somewhere along the way I lost myself. I had to find my way back to happiness and real love. I felt guilty for thinking about Kanye. He was heavy on my mind and hard to shake off. I looked over at Smooth and I'm not going to lie I have very little love left for him inside my heart. This relationship was definitely hanging by a thread and the only reason that I'm still with him is because of the children. It was getting late so I had to force myself to sleep. Tomorrow I will go by and visit my mother and talk about doing counseling with me. After that I will swing by my mother in law house too. It's been a very long time since I've seen her and that's not like us to not keep in touch with one another. I laid down on Smooth's chest and dozed off to sleep.

Smooth

The next morning I was awakened by the smell of breakfast. Ciara was standing over me smiling, holding a tray of food. On the tray my plate was filled with French toast, rice, bacon, eggs, and fresh squeezed orange juice.

"Good morning." Ciara smiled and said. She looked radiant and fresh as she set the tray across from me. I sat up and she kissed me on the cheek. Playfully I turned the side of my face so that she could kiss me on the mouth. "Ughhh, morning breath." Ciara said. I laughed and ate my breakfast, turned on the television to channel nine news. The breaking news was the number of shootings that were occurring throughout Chicagoland. That's why I stayed strapped at all times because this was murder capital and fuck niggas didn't want to work hard for shit. Instead they wanted to take yours. My phone rang and it was Kayla calling me. I looked down and debated if I should answer. I could hear the children screaming for Ciara's help downtown stairs, so I answered.

"What Kayla?" I asked.

"My daughter is what's up! How has she been doing?" She asked.

"Our daughter is doing fine. She's in good hands and I told you to call my mother instead. She could tell you more than I can being that she's living with her."

"Oh it's our daughter now. The DNA test results came back saying that you are the father. I told you that from the jump that Variyah was your baby girl. Anyway, I know that she lives with your mom but have you been spending time with her like a father is supposed to do?" Kayla asked.

"Look don't question my father skills, I'm doing a great job at that. You just work on your mommy skills. Why do you always have to call and start bullshit all the time? Why can't we never have a peaceful conversation?" I asked.

"Because shit isn't peaceful at all Smooth as long as I'm inside here. I miss my baby girl so much, you hiding her and me from your bitch, and you talk to me any type of way. Don't worry it will be all over soon. I'm counting down the days and when I get out all hell is going to break loose."

"Kayla, you aren't crazy and I'm not concerned about you. My only concern is Variyah and if you don't watch who you're talking to I will make it that you will never see her again. Don't you ever disrespect my woman! Ciara hasn't done shit to you if you're mad at anyone it should be me. As far as me talking to you crazy that's only because you start tripping and if I don't do something about it then you will become a problem. I'm not one of them soft men who can't keep his chick in check so when you start showing me that you know how to act I will treat you different. You're hardhead, talk back too much, and never want to listen." I said.

"Damn baby daddy, so you going to threaten me with my daughter? Typical of you to do such a thing but trust and believe I'm not worry about that, period! Ha! Ha! Ha! The listen time that I listened to you I ended up in here. I'm not one of them chicks that you could run anymore and tell what to do. Smooth, you better be ready because once I step out this bitch it's a whole new world. I'm going to call and check on my baby girl and stop wasting my calls on your sorry ass," said Kayla.

"Aye Kayla girl, you need to chill the fuck out for real." I said but Kayla had already hung up the phone. I couldn't even eat my damn breakfast in peace. Every time she calls she is on one and always popping off at the mouth. I can't wait till she gets out so I could fuck her up because she's acting out of her body. Ciara came back inside the room and looked down at my plate and looked back at me.

"What's wrong you didn't like my cooking this morning?" She asked being concerned with why I haven't eaten all of my food.

"Nah baby, you on point, I got a phone from my mother and started talking with her." I lied.

"Speaking of your mother, I think I will swing by her place today and give her a visit. I haven't seen her in a while." Ciara said.

Damn, why did I say that I was talking to my mother, I thought to myself, *I could've said Vell, Red, or even Ant. Now I opened up another can of worms that I can't get myself out of.* I couldn't stop my girl from going to my mom house that would be suspicious. I already had to lie about the baby last night. If Ciara see that baby, she would flip out because she resembles me. I had to think of something quick.

"Call and make sure that she will be there first. I think she said that she was stepping out for a little while today." I said.

"Okay, I will do that. Do you want me to take the food away?" Ciara asked.

I had loss my appetite this morning so I told her to take it away. As soon as she went down stairs and it was safe to call my mother, I did just that.

"Hey Ma, Ciara is going to call you today and ask to come over and visit. Can you do your son a favor and tell her that you won't be at home today?" I asked my mother.

"Smooth, you still haven't told her about Variyah? Fool what has gotten into you? The children played and held their baby sister yesterday. I'm surprised that they haven't told her. I'm going to this last favor for you, but you have a week to tell her and if you don't I will. I can't continue to keep covering for you." My mother talked loudly into the phone.

"Thank you Mom I will pay you back I promise. I have to go now because Ciara is coming back upstairs, I love you." I said.

"I love you too Eric, good bye." My mom hung up.

Ciara walked back in the room and I got up to get in the shower. While showering I could hear Ciara on the phone talking with my mom. From the conversation it sounded like the plan had went through. Ten minutes later I got out and dressed for the day. Ciara and the children were downstairs and ready to go out the door.

"Hey baby, the kids and I are going to spend some time at my mother's house. I was going to swing by your mom's house, but she said that she had some errands to run. I was thinking for dinner the kids and I could meet you at Olive Garden this evening." Ciara said.

"That's fine baby." I said kissing all three of them. "I will call and let you know when to meet me. Tell your mother that I said hello as well."

"Alright we gone and you be safe out there in them streets. I love you."

I helped Ciara put the children inside the car and kissed her one more time before she pulled off. I went back inside and made sure that I had my piece on me. Today was Saturday and I know it was going to be crazy out. I had to meet up at the trap house to have a meeting with the fellas. When I got there, everyone was there and Vell had already started. Last week one of our workers had got stuck up for half a bird. He didn't see who the people were because they had on mask. I was pissed because this was my first time hearing about it. I know that I haven't been in the streets lately and have been spending more time at home with my family. The meeting went on for another twenty minutes before wrapping up. Ant was talking about gambling as usual and wanted to go to Indiana. I didn't mind blowing off some steam on the crap table and winning some money so we all decided to head over to the Horseshoe. Ant made himself-comfortable at the blackjack table. We were all drinking and sitting in the bar then this brown skinned chick walked over to Vell and gave him a kiss. We all sat back and looked well except for Ant he was busy winning. Vell introduced her as his girl Vicky, it dawned on me that it was shorty from the hotel that he had with him. When Vicky excused herself to go to the washroom, we took Vell ass down.

"Damn Vell, where you find little from? She slugging." Red said.

"She lives next door to me. Well Aaliyah put me out so I got another place last week ago." Vell said.

"Damn you banging your next door neighbor? How that hell that started?" asked Red.

"Man she always flirted with a player one day I decided to give it a try. Ever since that I couldn't stop, it's like she got me hooked or something," said Vell.

"I didn't know Aaliyah put you out." I said.

"Yes I accidently called her by mistake when I was fucking Vicky. She heard everything and flipped out and put a player out. The good thing about it all is that she doesn't know that it was Vicky," said Vell.

"Damn boy, you better hope that she don't find out either because Aaliyah's crazy ass will the both of you. Real talk, she isn't wrapped to tight." Red laughed and while drinking his drink.

"She already tripping by not letting me see the twins. I have to go up to their school to see them. I swear she's blowing me with that bullshit right there because they don't have nothing to do with it. My daughters miss the hell out of me. They always ask when I'm coming back home. I just tell them real soon." Vell said.

Ant came over to join us finally after he left the table. You could tell by the look on his face that he lost his money. He ordered a drink and pulled out his cigar and puffed on it.

"Those pussy muther fuckers took all my money. Aye Vell look behind you, there goes Aaliyah." Ant said jokily puffing on his cigar. Vell looked scared as hell looking over his shoulder. We all laughed so hard.

"Stop playing man, you better win that money back before Kelly fuck you up while you over there laughing." Vell said.

"Aye that's the plan play boy, I didn't come to this muther fucker to lose. I'm winning all my shit back!" Ant said.

Vicky walked back up and sat down next to Vell. She ordered herself and drink and crossed her legs. She whispered something in Vell's ear and that nigga got the cheesing so hard. Red, Ant, and I left the two alone and went to gamble. Ant pulled out another wad of money, I swear the man had a gambling problem. Two hours later I was ready to go. Red and I broke even, Ant won his money back and few extra bucks. Vell and his girl had plans, he was sloppy drunk. He rode back with Vicky, we made sure that he was straight. We all jumped in the car and hit the eway. My voicemail alert went off several indicating that I had messages. I never got service when I was on the boat I had T Mobile, the shittest provider. I called Ciara back and explained to her that I was on the boat and didn't have any service. She checked my ass and told me to meet her and the children at Olive Garden in an hour. Red got me back to my car and I had fifth teen minutes to make it to Ciara. I checked on my workers first to make sure that they were straight. Everyone was cool but I told them to call me if anything pops out. I put extra security on the block that stick up shit was on my mind. I hopped in my whip and push the pedal to the metal all the way to the Olive Garden. Ciara and the children was sitting at the table eating already once I got there.

"Hey baby, I'm sorry for running late." I kissed her and my children.

"No problem it's fine I ordered your favorite because I knew that you would be running late as usual." Ciara said as she signaled the waiter to bring my plate. The waiter arrived with my food and Ciara updated me on her day.

"My mon will be going to my next counseling session with me. I'm looking forward to how this will turn out," said Ciara.

"I think that is a good idea and would be great. You two have a lot to talk about during that situation." I said.

"Yes it's a lot of things that haven't been discussed on my end and need to be addressed. It's about time that I and my mother discuss some issues."

My cell phone rang and it was Kayla calling me. I sent her to the voicemail, but she called back again. Ciara busied herself with Eric Jr. and wiped his hands and mouth. Kayla didn't care that I was ignoring her call and called back several times again. It was annoying as hell.

"Who is that and why aren't you answering your phone?" Ciara asked.

"It's a private caller and I don't answer private calls." I said.

Ciara rolled her eyes and was about to say something smart out her mouth but my phone rang again. She quickly picked it up with a frown on her face.

"Hello, oh hey Vell. I'm fine and he's sitting right next to me. Here it's Vell." Ciara handed me my phone and

I was too happy that it wasn't Kayla calling. I was so happy that I didn't even want to check her ass for answering my phone. Vell hollered at me on the phone and Kayla's crazy ass continued to keep calling me on the other line. When I got off the phone with him, I blocked Kayla's number. I didn't have time for immature ass. She was going to make me fuck her ass up.

Chapter Seven

Kelly

I was out school for the week, but I return back next week for only two days and then after that I was graduating. I needed this time off because lately I have been running around crazy during the day and at night I would be too exhausted to please my man. Ant and I were laying back, chilling, and smoking. For the first day off we planned on staying inside, turning off the phones, and enjoying one another. Between the both of our lives it was hectic so this time being alone was much needed. We notified our family and friends ahead of time and told them to notify us only in case of an emergency. So far everything was peaceful. The ceiling fan spun and the breeze hit my nipples making them hard.

"Bae, do you think I will look cute with my nipples pierced? I'm thinking about getting them pierced?" I asked Ant.

"Leave my pretty breasts alone. Don't mess them up with all that bullshit. Your body is perfect, you don't need any tattoos or nothing." Ant said puffing on the blunt.

"What you mean your breasts?" I asked him playfully slapping his right hand away. Anthony passed me the blunt and rubbed on my breast. I hit the blunt as Ant sucked on my perky breast. The circles of smoke danced in the air as he kissed and licked on my breast.

"Baby, you know how much I love you. Your body is so perfect that I wouldn't change a thing about you. I'm a lucky man to have you. You're smart, beautiful, and strong." Ant kissed my neck softly getting me aroused.

"You trying to start something, stick it in bae. I'm hot and ready." I whispered in his ear.

Ant slipped inside my wet pussy, I dug my nails into his back as he went deep inside me. We were caught in the moment when someone rang our doorbell. **Ding dong, dink dong.**

"Who in the hell is ringing the doorbell?!" I said getting up to answer the door.

I grabbed my terry cloth robe and threw it on. I marched to the door and opened it, there was an older light skinned woman standing outside my door. Her hair was brown with blond highlights. She was wearing big sunglasses that covered her face. I don't know who the hell she was ringing my doorbell.

"How can I help you?!" I asked her.

"Hello I'm looking for Anthony." The woman said.

"Who are you and why are you looking for Anthony?!" I asked.

The woman smiled, "You must be Kelly, nice to meet you." She said as she extended her hand out so that I could shake it. She realized that wasn't going to happen and removed her sunglasses. "I'm Marilyn, Anthony's mother."

I stared at her and now that I could see her face I can see the resemblance. "Anthony, can you please come to the door?!" I yelled. I wasn't going to let this strange woman in for all I know he maybe didn't want to see her. Ant came to the door and by the look on his face I could tell that he wasn't too happy to see her.

"Marilyn, what are you doing here?" He asked.

"Hey son aren't you happy to see me? You just going to leave me out here, do you have the decency to invite me in?" She asked.

"Kelly, she's cool let her in." He said. I moved out of the way and allowed her to walk in.

Marilyn walked in and looked around our home. From the way she was dressed she looked like the type of woman who thought she was still young. She had on a two piece legging outfit and high heels with a Gucci purse on her arm. I eyed her up and down and could tell that she was about to beg.

"Anthony, your grandmother told me where you lived, so I thought that I'd give you a visit. I hope that I didn't interrupt anything." She said smiling looking as though she could tell we were in the middle of having sex.

"So you decided to pop up to my place without giving me a call first? The last time I heard from you, you were living in Minnesota." Ant said.

"I left Minnesota it wasn't anything happening there so I decided to leave. I came back to Chicago last week. I'm staying with a friend until I get my own place. I miss you son, can I have a hug?"

Anthony walked away and sat down on the couch. I was waiting for him to give me the okay to put her out. From the stories that he shared with me, his mother wasn't really there for him. Much like my mother wasn't there for me either, that's why we had so much love for one another. All of the childhood pain that we endured from our parents being absent in our lives made us stronger. Marilyn sat down next to him and I walked off giving the two of them their privacy. Ant told me stay so I took a seat right next to him. I could tell that it was about to get real and you know that I had my man back.

"This is how you treat your mother that you haven't seen in three years? Despite everything that has happened in the past, I'm still your mother. I love and miss you, it hasn't been a day that I haven't stop thinking about you," said Marilyn.

"How much money do you need Marilyn? That is the only time that you come around and run back to your family." Ant asked.

"I didn't come here for money. I came here to see my son. I heard that you have a beautiful girlfriend and that the two of you are going to get married soon. I wanted to meet my daughter. Hello honey, nice to meet you." She said.

"Hi. I'm Kelly. Nice to meet you." I said being short with my comment.

Anthony was mad. I have never seen him so upset like this before. Yes, he was angry when he was set up and kidnapped last year, but right now this was a different type of mad that he displayed. The look on his face was the look of hate. I wasn't really feeling where this was going. Marilyn blew my high by interrupting us.

"Marilyn, there isn't any need of introducing yourself when you aren't going to stay around in the first place. All you ever did was run in and out of my life. I'm curious to see how long you plan on staying this time."

"Anthony, I just came by to visit my son and to see how he's doing. I could see that I'm not welcome so I will see myself out." Marilyn got up and walked toward the door.

"Marilyn, please don't go." I said quickly.

"Kelly don't stop her from leaving. Let her go she's good at doing that," said Ant.

Marilyn walked out of the door looking back at Anthony with a sad look upon her face. She rushed back to her car quickly and I got up to run after her in my terry cloth robe and house shoes. I felt bad about what just happen.

"Marilyn please wait a second, I want to apologize for Anthony's behavior." I said.

"Oh it's no problem besides if I was him I would be upset too. Kelly, it was nice meeting you." She said and drove off. I went back in the house and Ant was sitting on the couch rolling another blunt. He acted as though nothing has just happened as he lit the blunt and took a pull.

"You didn't have to treat her like that. Ant what's up?" I asked him.

"Kelly, I don't want to talk about it right now."

"I think the way that you treated her was mean."

"She's good at playing the victim all the time. Kelly just don't get involved."

"If you don't want me to get involved, then I won't. I have more important things to worry about like my graduation and wedding. Anyway can we get back to what we were doing?"

I dropped my robe and exposed my naked body giving Ant a tease. He got up and chased me around the house and caught me in the hallway throwing me against the wall. Three hours later we had made love all over the house just like we used to do when I first met him. We took a break to eat and ordered pizza and wings. We smoked again until the food arrived. Anthony received a phone call from his grandmother. I listened as he spoke with her about his mom. Once the food arrived we ate and then I jumped in the shower. Ant showered with me but didn't seem too much like himself after he received the phone call from his grandma. I asked him if everything was alright and he assured me that he was fine. I been with him for too long not to know that something was bothering my man.

The next morning I woke up to the smell of food cooking. My stomach was growling and I was starving. I rolled over to an empty spot in the bed where Ant usually lays. I smiled because my man was in the kitchen cooking me some breakfast. Last night was mad real after we ate we drank a bottle of Patron, smoked, and made love again. I was the first to pass out because the last thing I could remember was Ant and I falling out of bed while we were making love. I threw on my bra and boy shorts and made my way to the kitchen. I walked down the long hallway and skipped down the stairs.

"Good morning." I smiled but quickly my smile disappeared. Anthony and his mother were sitting at the kitchen table laughing and eating. They both stopped and stared at me as I stood in my underwear. I was so embarrassed that I ran back upstairs with Ant running behind me. When he made it to the bedroom, he was laughing so hard but I didn't think that shit was funny.

"Ain't nothing funny Ant! What is she doing her so damn early in the morning? I thought that you were cooking me breakfast. Stop laughing." I said while I threw on some sweats.

"Ha! Ha! Ha! Be cool Kelly, Marilyn called me early this morning and asked if she could come over and cook us breakfast." Ant said still laughing.

"Yesterday you threw her out of our home. Today she's in our kitchen, I'm lost Ant. What the hell is really going on?" I asked.

"After my grandma got in my ass about the way that I treated her I have to be nice. You know how much I love my granny and does whatever she says."

"I feel so embarrassed. Next time you better tell me when we have company. You know how I like to walk around naked." I said.

"You good baby, now let's go downstairs and have some breakfast." Ant said.

We went back down and Marilyn was sitting down eating. "I apologize Marilyn I didn't know that you were here." I said.

"Oh it's okay babe. I totally understand and I want to apologize about popping up yesterday unannounced. That wasn't cool." Marilyn said.

"Alright enough with all the apologizing, can we all eat now?" Ant said.

Marilyn and I laughed and began to eat. The omelet was really good and so were the homemade waffles. Ant and his mom talked and shared old memories. I would chime in from time to time but wasn't really feeling this. In the back of my mind I wanted to know what her reason was for this unexpected visit. She rubbed me the wrong way and seemed shady. I was going to find out what was her motive.

It was Wednesday, day three of my week off and Marilyn was still around. I know the plan was to stay inside and for Ant and I have to some alone time but those plans has changed. I had to get out of this house before I snapped out. I called Ciara and told her that I was on my way to the boutique. I got dressed and when I left out Ant and Marilyn were sitting in the living room on the couch playing the game. Ant was surprised to see me dressed.

"Where are you going baby looking so damn good?" asked Ant.

"I'm going to hang out with Ciara for a couple of hours." I said.

"Cool. I was hoping that tonight we all can go out to eat. Me, you, and Marilyn for dinner."

"Sounds good, I will love too." I gave Ant a hug and several kisses before leaving. He smacked me on my butt and told me that he loved me. I said see you later to him and Marilyn and left out of the door. It didn't take too long to get to the boutique. When I arrived Ciara had a few customers. I spoke to everyone and went to have a sit in

Ciara's office in the back. I noticed that she had her office redecorated and it looked nice. The walls were purple and yellow with a purple shag rug on the floor. Her black wooden desk wasn't too big nor too small. It was just right with her Apple laptop and printer. She had a painting of her on the wall, several vases and a purple cute loveseat with yellow throw pillows. I made myself comfortable while I waited for her to take a break. Ten minutes later Ciara was free to talk and walked in.

"What's up friend? I thought that you and Ant was going to be booed up and wasn't going to be available this week. Girl, I have so much to tell you." Ciara said.

"Girl, I thought so too, that was until his mother popped up and ruined everything. I'm talking about it feels like she just dropped from the sky. I know you have a lot to tell me, but I have to go first." I said.

"Oh wow I'm surprised because I thought that Ant and his mom didn't rock like that."

"They didn't at first but as of now they're the best of friends. Let me fill you in real quick on everything. Monday she shows up on our doorstep and Ant wasn't too happy to see her. She invites herself in and they both go back and forth to the point that she leaves because she doesn't like how Ant is treating her. Later that night Ant's grandmother called him and got in his ass about it so he has a change of heart. Tuesday morning she's cooking breakfast for us. Tuesday afternoon she leaves and comes back with gifts." I said but Ciara cut me off.

"Girl are you serious? What do you mean by gifts?" Ciara asked.

"You know Ant plays his videos games. She bought him several games for his Xbox and PlayStation. Designer clothes and shoes and guess what she bought me? Bitch do you see this Chanel bag, she bought this for me and yes it's real. You and I both know Chanel isn't cheap." I said.

"That bag is nice! It's the new one, she had to spend a grip on that. Where is she getting her money from?" Ciara asked.

"See that's what I'm trying to figure out as well. At first Ant and I thought that maybe she was coming back around to beg and ask for some money like she has in the past. From the looks of things she doesn't seem to have money problems."

"How does she look? You don't think she's selling pussy? I hate to say that but whatever she's doing I'm quite sure that it's illegal." said Ciara.

"She's actually not a bad looking woman for her age. Marilyn is in good shape, she has all of her teeth, and she keeps herself up. You know she always felt like she was younger and never really hung around women her age. I don't think that she is a hoe or anything. Whatever she's doing or who she's involved with, they are definitely checking plenty of cash." I said.

"I'm more than sure that you will find out. What's done in the dark always comes to light. You just be on your shit and watch everything. I know that is his mother and all but you have to keep in mind that her popping up with money does seem a little suspicious." Ciara said.

"You know I am, tonight we are all going out to eat and after that I'm going to have a talk with Ant about everything."

"Yes you do that and keep it real with him. Let me tell you about last week. Smooth and I had went to counseling. At first it didn't off too well but ended out good. Tomorrow my mom and I are going back, but you won't believe who is my therapist. Take a wild guess friend, you and I both know her." Ciara said smiling.

"Girl who? Tell me." I said smiling back.

"Mrs. Wilson from the group home," said Ciara.

"Really that's great. I'm so happy that you're finally getting the help that you need. I like how Smooth and your mom is supporting you and if you ever need me to be there for you, I will be. You know last year you kept me busy watching over you. I was really concerned about you because we had lost Jasmine to suicide then he you come with the drinking. I honestly thought that I was going to lose you too. Sis, I can't do this alone. I need you by my side for whatever." I choked up a bit and a tear rolled down my right cheek. Ciara got up from her seat and sat next to me on the couch.

"Kelly, you know you're all that I have after all the bullshit and the smoke clears. You have been there ever since the beginning so you know my past. I want to say thank you for always keeping it real and being on my ass when it came to the drinking situation. Girl, I was losing myself and you were there to pick me up when I was falling. I got your back and we are going to get to the bottom of Marilyn's ass. If she on some bullshit and trying to bring some chaos and confusion in your life, you know I have no problem helping you send her back from where she came from. Give me hug and sis, and we going to stop all this crying." Ciara said.

"It's just really crazy now with me graduating next week and planning a wedding. It's like everything is happening so fast."

"I got you and everything is going to be fine. I can't wait to see you walk across that stage." Ciara said giving me a hug.

I wiped away my tears and Ciara and I changed the subject. I hung around the boutique until they closed allowing Ant and his mom to bond. I made it back to the house to shower and change before we headed out for dinner. We went out to eat at Ruth Chis Steakhouse. Miss big baller shot caller told us that we could have anything to eat on the menu. I had no problem with that and ordered a bottle of white wine. I guess she wanted to make up for all the moments for not being around in Anthony's life. Marilyn told us that her friend would be joining us soon so we waited a moment to order our food until her friend arrived. I was sipping on my glass of wine and I noticed a younger man walked up to our table. Marilyn smiled and the younger man gave her a kiss on the lips. I damn near choked on my wine as I looked over at Ant who looked confused just like me. Marilyn seen the looks on the both of our faces and introduced us to her friend.

"Kelly and Anthony this is my friend Lorenzo. Lorenzo this is my son, Anthony, and his lovely fiancé, Kelly." Marilyn said.

"Hello Anthony nice to finally meet you. I heard so much about you." Lorenzo said shaking Anthony's hand.

119

He spoke to me as well and I said hello smiling thinking in my head what is Marilyn doing with this fine ass man? He was fresh too, looking like money, and that Rolex was standing out on his wrist. He looked like he could be in his early thirties, which was young beings that Marilyn was fifty one. He sat down next to Marilyn and the waiter came over to take our order. I looked over at my man and could tell that he was pissed but taking it really cool. I grabbed his hand and whispered in his ear.

"Take it easy and let's just enjoy the meal. Talk to her about it later." I said.

"Ok babe, but I know this cat from somewhere." Ant said giving me a kiss.

You can tell that Marilyn and Lorenzo had to be dealing with one another for quite some time from the way they both carried on at the table. Dinner was going great until Ant busted out where he knew him from. We all were in the middle of eating and conversing.

"You wouldn't happen to be Lorenzo who cracks cards?" Ant asked.

I starting coughing and grabbed my chest. "Ant be cool, not in the restaurant." I said.

"Anthony, please don't start." Marilyn said.

"I am that Lorenzo and aren't ashamed at what I do. Just like you are Ant who sells dope, correct?" Lorenzo said.

"Okay it's time to go." I grabbed Ant by the hand and was about to get up to leave but Ant didn't move.

"You right that's me and I am not knocking your hustle at all, just don't get my mother caught in your bullshit in the process." Ant said.

"I will never do no such thing. I really care about your mother." Lorenzo said.

"Yes son, he really does and takes real good care of me." Marilyn said.

Anthony looked like he wanted to kill some shit right now. I was holding both of his hands so that he wouldn't swing on Lorenzo and knock his ass out. He told me to let his hands go and that it was time for to leave. He got up and walked out of the restaurant holding my hand. I said goodbye to Marilyn and Lorenzo before leaving. We waited outside for the valet to bring our car around. Ant remained quiet the entire ride home. I was scared to say something. Once we got inside, Marilyn had called him several times, but he didn't answer. I rubbed his shoulders as he set up in the bed thinking. His other phone rang and it was Smooth calling. Ant took the call and walked out of the room. I never heard him talk business that was between him and his guys. I chilled out and watched a movie waiting on him to come back in the room. His other phone rang again and it was Marilyn calling, I answered it.

"Hello." I said.

"Hey Kelly, I take it that Anthony is upset with me and don't really feel like talking too me." Marilyn said.

"Just give him some time he's still trying to register everything that happened tonight. Marilyn, it would've help if you would've told him ahead of time." I said defending my man.

"You're right Kelly I should've told him about Lorenzo before all of us having dinner together. I messed up and I really don't want my son cutting me back off again. We were back bonding and getting along." She said.

"Everything will be fine. I will have a talk with him, don't worry about nothing. Get you some rest." I said.

"Please handle it Kelly. Goodnight." Marilyn hung up the phone.

I placed Ant's phone back on the bed and he walked back in feeling a little bit better. He must have heard some good news from Smooth. His mood had changed and he scooped me in his arms and kissed me deeply.

"Kelly right now it's all about me and you. Fuck all that dumb shit that happened tonight. If my mother is happy, I'm happy. If it wasn't for you, I would've fucked dude up. You keep me sane and I love you." Ant said.

"I love you too, daddy, and it's me and you against the world." I said

Anthony laid me down and undressed me. I was ready to end this night the right way. We were naked in a matter of seconds and exploring one another. In the middle of making love, the doorbell rang. Ant and I ignored it and then his phone rang. It was Marilyn, but we ignored it. She began yelling his name, but we ignored her. Shortly after she went away, we never stopped our love making. I loved Ant and he loved me. It was me and him against anyone or anything that was creating drama.

Graduation Day

I sat in my seat wearing my cap and gown and watching my fellow classmates walk across the stage. I was waiting patiently for the speaker to call my name. I couldn't believe this day had finally come. I worked so hard day and night, stayed out of the parties, and out of the bullshit. I remained focused on my goal and just wanted something out of life. I was determined to make it out of the hood and take care of my grandmother. Today was the day I was waiting for. It was time and our stood up and waited for our names to be announced. The crowd cheered each time someone received their degree. I was up next and the last to be called the speaker of the house said my name.

"Last but certainly not least, Kelly White." I walked across the stage as my family and friends cheered for me. I shook the speakers' hand and fell out on the stage and screamed, "Yes!"

Everyone stood up and clapped. I heard my brother Shawn call out my name. Tears of joy fell out my eyes. The Class of 2014 had officially graduated and the ceremony was over. I made my way through the crowd to get to my family. I was a few times to take pictures with some of my classmates. I finally found my family and friends and ran straight to my grandmother and hugged her.

"Kelly, I'm so proud of you. I prayed for this day, God is good!" My grandmother said.

Everyone was there, Anthony, and his friends Smooth, Red, and Vell. Ciara, Niecy, and my brother Shawn. A few more of my relatives were there as well. Everyone gave me flowers, cards, and money. We all went back to my grandmother's house where Shawn had food catered for my celebration. He didn't want her cooking at all. We had a lot of food and few of Anthony's family members came by as well. I stepped outside on the back to talk to my brother alone.

"I'm very proud of you little sis. I have a gift for you." Shawn went inside his pocket and gave me $5,000 dollars.

"What's all this for? You know I don't need your money, Shawn. You have done more than enough by paying for my schooling, buying me a car, and putting money in my pocket."

"You know that I have to make sure that you're straight. So tell me, little sis, what's your next plan?" Shawn asked.

"I'm going to find a job and I would like to go back for my Masters in Finance." I said.

"That's good and I will support you in whatever you decide to do." Shawn said giving me a hug.

"You know I really miss Jasmine and wish that she was here." I said walking back inside the house.

"Yes me too, I miss her like crazy. I have an idea me, you, and Ciara should go get tattoos done in her memory." Shawn said.

"That's cool and I will tell Ciara." I said.

I talked to Ciara about getting a tattoo in Jasmine's memory and she was down. I had to ask Ant if it was cool that I get one because he did say that he didn't want me to tat my body. He thought that it was cool and had no problem with me getting one as long as it wasn't on my breast. I wouldn't get 'RIP Jasmine' tatted on my breast anyway. My graduation party went on all night and Marilyn showed up to give her support. Ant wasn't mad at her any longer and was happy to see her. My grandmother yelled for me to come and get the house phone. When I got on the phone, it was mother calling collect from prison. I haven't talked or seen her in a while. I knew that she was going to call me and I was happy that she did.

"Hey baby girl, Congratulations! I'm so proud of you and I wish that I could've been there to watch you walk across that stage. I told everyone in here that you were graduating today. You know I love bragging about you. Kelly, I remember the day that you were born and I laid eyes on you I knew that you were going to be successful." My mother cried into the phone.

"Thank you mama, I really wish that you could be here as well. I really miss you and I'm sorry that I've ignored your calls and haven't come to visit you. I'm going to do better at doing that. Enough about me, how are you?" I said.

"I'm fine, baby girl, you know your brother keeps my commissary full. I'm in the process of writing a book right now. You brother is going to connect me with a publisher that he knows. I'm so excited because you know that your mother has a story to tell."

"That's great and you know I will help you out with anything. I'm glad to hear you sounding better than the last time that I spoke with you. Ant said hello by the way, he's right here kissing all on my neck." I said.

"You two love birds, tell my son that I said what's up and that I love him. Where is Shawn? Baby girl, can you put him on the phone real quick? I need to holler at him before I go, we about to go on lockdown."

I called Shawn to come to the phone and he went to the bedroom to talk with my mother on the phone in private. We turned up the music and my little cousin was trying to teach me all the latest dances that were out. I couldn't do any of those new dances, but Ciara was good at it. I was like enough of all that fast music and we turned on slow music. Ant and I were slow dancing to Avant's song, My First Love while everyone watched us.

"I'm so proud of you baby and I love you so much!" Ant whispered in my ear.

"I love you more." I said.

All of a sudden my grandmother fell out on the floor and everyone rushed over to help her. She was still breathing but it was shallow. I cried hysterically and Ciara called 911. The paramedics made it in ten minutes and took her to Cook County Hospital. We all followed them and Ant comforted me while we waited for the doctors to tell us what was going on. For the first time in a long time, I prayed to God like never before.

Chapter Eight

Cherish

The fresh air hit me and the sun shone brightly in my face. I felt like I was in heaven but I wasn't dead, more like born again now that I was a free woman. I was so anxious to see my baby girl Laniyah. Lorenzo sat outside in the parked car with Laniyah strapped in her car seat in the back. I jumped in the car and sat in the back seat on the ride home. Once we made it in the house Lorenzo ran me some water in our Jacuzzi tub. I soaked and enjoyed the powerful jets that hit my body. The water felt amazing, it has been a year since I've taken a bath. As I soaked I thought about getting back on my grind and making my money. Forty minutes later I was ready to get out. Laniyah's baby cries made me move a little faster. Quickly, I wrapped a towel around my body and went to her room to find her daddy holding her in his arms. Lorenzo looked up at me and smiled.

"She's cool, look at you coming to her rescue. You look good Cherish." Lorenzo said.

"Thank you and so do you, it's something different about you," I said looking into his eyes.

"Fatherhood will change a man," said Lorenzo.

I sat down next to him, Lorenzo passed me Laniyah. She looked into my eyes and smiled. A tear dropped from my eye and trickled down my cheek.

"Hey princess mommy is home and I'm not going to leave you anymore. I'm going to spoil you rotten and protect you. I miss you so much." I said smothering her with kisses.

"I'm going to take care of the both of you. I'm so happy that you're finally home. While you were away, Laniyah reminded me some much of you." Lorenzo said.

Quietly, I rocked Laniyah back to sleep. She wasn't ready to wake up in the first place. Ten minutes later she was sleep and I laid her down in the crib. Lorenzo was busy talking on the phone in his office. I went to our bedroom and applied baby oil to my body. I noticed the numerous of gifts that were scattered across my bed. I opened one after the other to find lingerie, clothes, shoes, jewelry, and a shoe box full of money. It felt like Christmas in July. Lorenzo was now standing at the door watching me.

"Thank you babe, everything is so nice. What else do you have for me?" I asked him wrapping my arms around his neck. He eyed my nude body up and down and licked his lips while rubbing my juicy ass. I was ready for him to lay that pipe in me and bang my pussy up. We kissed and Lorenzo ushered me to the bed pushing all the items on the floor. He tossed my naked body onto the bed, my legs were cocked opened waiting for his arrival. I cupped my right breast, licking and sucking on it. I fingered my pussy with my left hand as Lorenzo watched and quickly undressed. He tasted my sweet peach and I pushed his head into my pussy deeper. Oh I missed his tongue so much, it felt so good that it didn't take long for me to explode in his mouth. "Oh my god I miss you so damn much." I moaned in his ear.

I aggressively threw him on the bed and pounced on top of him. My pussy was so wet that he slipped right inside me. I bounced up and down on his dick. "Oh shit!" said Lorenzo. He grabbed my hips and thrust his dick inside of me fucking me back. I screamed, "Oh please don't stop, give me all you got!" Lorenzo went faster and faster causing me to howl. Our sex voices woke Laniyah, she began to cry but we didn't stop until we reached our peak. It didn't take long for Lorenzo to release and bust. I hopped off of his dick fast because I didn't want him shooting inside me. I don't have time to be walking around here pregnant and having more babies. The only thing that I wanted to be making more of was money. I put on my robe and quickly went to see about Laniyah who was now screaming at the top of her lungs.

"What's the matter? Mommy and daddy is so sorry that we woke you up." Laniyah continued to cry. Once that smell hit my nose I knew why she was crying. I changed my baby diaper, I couldn't believe that something like that could come out of her. I sprayed the air fresher after I was done. Laniyah and I went to the kitchen and I made her a bottle. She sure was hungry because it didn't take long for her to drink an eight ounce bottle. I burped her and we went to go see what her daddy was doing. Lorenzo was busy in his at home office on the laptop. I sat down in the chair along with Laniyah sitting in my lap.

"So what's going on? Fill me in on everything." I said.

"Right now money is flowing in like crazy. I have my team of people getting others to flip their money left and right." Lorenzo said.

"That's cool how are you able to do that? Where are you finding these people?" I asked.

"From off social media. It's easy we make fake pages, post pictures of people living good, and flashing cash enticing several people. The people reach out to us and I ask them if they want to flip $200 into $2000. They say yes and ask what do they have to do? That's when I find out if they have an active checking account and make sure that it isn't negative. I tell them the plan, they give up their cards. The fake checks are made and deposited into their accounts. Once the check clears in the morning, we go and get the money out and give them their cut. We try to flip as many checks that the bank allows." Lorenzo said.

"So you trying to tell me that some people are just that stupid to let you do that? That's cool with but damn talking about just plain dumb." I said.

"People are greedy and don't want to work too hard for nothing now a days." Lorenzo said.

He continued to talk and explain everything to me. I listened because I was about to build a team of my own and get this money. Even though Lorenzo had given me some money I still had to make my own. Plus I have a child now so I needed to put money up for her as well. We couldn't depend on Lorenzo and yes I know that he loved me without a doubt but ain't nothing like your own. Lorenzo busied himself with his work. I went to Laniyah's room to bond some more with her. We were watching the Disney channel and her eyes lit up at the screen. At three months she was very advanced rolling over and trying to sit and pull up on her own. She was active just like her mommy. I could tell that she was going to be a busy body. Once Lorenzo was done handling his business, he went to the kitchen to cook dinner. Yes my man could cook his ass off, so could I. During my incarceration we both agreed that once I was released that he would handle all the household things and that I would only have to focus on being a mother. I didn't have a problem with that and most women would love to have a man who caters to them. When I first met Lorenzo, I didn't have nothing, not a pot to piss in or a window to throw it out of. I dropped out of high school, ran away from home, and lived from one friend's house to another. My friend and I was shop lifting and boosting when I ran into him at the mall at the mall. He flirted, he looked good, was older, and most of all had money. At the time I was looking for someone to take care of me. He took me in and showed me how to get money the crooked way. Love came later on after he showed me how loyal he was. It was hard for me to trust people because all my life I've been played. After the money started flowing in everything was cool and going great that was until I got popped off and sent to jail. That came along with the game so I did my time and now my goal is to get back down. Lorenzo told me that dinner was done. He cooked Pepper Steak and Rice, my favorite. I loved how he had the bell peppers and onions chopped up just the right size. Lorenzo and I sat at the table eating, Laniyah was sitting in her bouncer that sat on the dining room table. I ate my food and sipped on my wine, the food was amazing.

"Thank you for making my favorite you don't know how much I miss a home cooked meal." I said stuffing the food down my mouth.

"Anything for you my queen. I want to make up the time that we loss. I hated that you carried my child while doing time. That shit tore me apart." Lorenzo said.

"It was hard and every day I remained strong for my child. I couldn't break down or let that get to me. Me being locked up while I was pregnant was awful but something good came out of it." I looked over at Laniyah who was now sleeping.

"That's our princess, she's beautiful just like you." Lorenzo said.

"Yes she looks just like me. Thank you for being there for me and for being faithful. A lot of men could never go without sex for a year."

"I love you baby and will never cheat on you."

I looked deep into his eyes and could see that something wasn't sincere. Maybe it was the wine that I was sipping that had me thinking extra.

The next day I was scheduled to get pampered. I stepped into 'Hot Topics Salon' and my stylist Brittany was so happy to see me.

"Oh my god Cherish I miss you girl. Welcome home! Look at you, you look great. Come on and let me get you started." Brittany said while giving me a hug.

I followed her to the shampoo bowl and said hello to the rest of the stylists and a few people that I know. I sat down, Brittany placed a towel around my neck and asked me to sit back so that she could wash my hair. I had to kick the conversation off and find out all the latest gossip. Brittany knew everything because everyone told her their business. She has been doing my hair for the last three years and we have become very close. Whatever I shared with her never got out so I trusted her with my business.

"Girl, tell me what has been going on since I've been gone?" I asked.

"You know the same old bullshit in Chicago. People getting shot and killed. This girl sleeping with that someone's husband or man. These men running around here sleeping with everyone, women and men included. Last but not least everyone is rich and getting money, flexing and showing out on the Instagram." Brittany said.

"Girl Lorenzo told me about Instagram and how people post all their business and life on there. That's crazy." I said.

"Yes people would sell their souls for some likes. Women posting naked pictures. Men posting pictures of money and guns. Girl it's just silly. I have a Instagram page but I use mine for promotional use only. Promoting only my salon and placing pictures of my clients." Brittany said.

"I tell you one thing you won't catch me on there doing any of that."

"Anyway how's the baby doing? I got a chance to meet her a couple of months ago when I ran into Lorenzo at Longhorn Steakhouse with baby. She's so pretty and looks just like you." Brittany said.

"Thank you she's doing great. I'm so happy to finally be home with her. I call her Princess Laniyah. So who was Lorenzo with when seen him and my baby in Longhorn?" I asked Brittany.

Brittany pretending like she didn't hear me and changed the subject trying to be slick. I caught on but wasn't letting that shit slide. I cut Brittany off in the middle of sentence talking about Beyoncé and Jay Z's daughter, who I clearly give a fuck about.

"Brittany don't play me. I asked who Lorenzo was with." I said.

"Cherish that really doesn't matter who he was with at the time because right now he's with you. Besides just because I saw him with another woman doesn't mean that they're messing around." Brittany said.

"Girl cut the bullshit and tell me before I act a fool in here." I warned.

"Okay! Damn he was with a woman named Marilyn. Now that you know you better not tell Lorenzo that I told you either. She's older and works with him, I know that they spend a lot of time together because I have seen them together on more than just one occasion." Brittany said.

"Since when have I ever told anyone that you told me anything when you tell me something? Brittany you know we go way back and if the shoe was on the other foot I would tell you if your man was chilling with another woman. Thanks for telling me and I will look into it and find out what's really going on. I'm not going to jump to any conclusions as of yet but I will get to the bottom of it." I said.

"Cool you do that and handle your business, but don't let that side track you from taking care of yours. You know men are going to be men and as women we have to learn to accept some things and remain in control of our feelings. Right now don't be concerned about what I just told you and focus on the fact that you just came home and that you have a baby girl to take care of. All that other shit is irrelevant." Brittany said.

"I feel you on that. I really can't be out here acting a fool but I'm not going to let anyone play me as such either. I'm done talking about it." I said.

Brittany remained quiet and started blow drying my hair. After she was done I talked about a few things because I didn't want her to feel uncomfortable and not be able to tell me anything else. She opened back up to me and conversed back with me. We were right back laughing and talking about everything just like the old days. I'm not going to lie I felt silly when I heard that shit when she told me, but I knew that something had to be going on when I was gone. You know the saying, 'When the cat is away, the mouse will play,' was very true because if I wasn't gone it wouldn't be another. Britany sewed in my hair, cut, and curled it. After she was done, she arched my brows and I was looking fabulous. I paid and tipped her. The nail technician was able to fit me in and gave me a no chip manicure and pedicure. I left the shop but before leaving I gave Brittany a hug assuring her that I wasn't upset. I felt back like the old Cherish, now all I needed to do was recruit me a new team. I could easily call up my old girls but I decided that I would start over all fresh. They all bailed off from me and didn't check on me while I was locked up so fuck them. As I was leaving out of the shop, a young girl with a baby on her hip and one holding another one's hand asked me if she could use my cell phone to call someone. From the looks of things she looked like that she needed some help. I let her use my phone and from the conversation she needed had a fight with her baby daddy. I felt sorry for her and offered her and her two kids a ride home. During the ride I asked if she wanted to make some money and she was down. After I told her everything and what I needed her to do she was ready to start right away. I liked to hear that because I knew that she wasn't lazy and ready to get this money. I gave her $100 dollars and told her that I would give her a call in the morning and to be ready. She was happy and promised that she would be and was waiting for my call. Okay I had one girl for now and that's cool because that's all I really needed at the moment. I still had Kayla who was ready too once she got out. I went home to my family and decided not to bring this Marilyn woman up right now. I had to get my money right first and if Lorenzo is messing with her I will shit on the both of them at the end.

Chapter Nine

Ciara

My mom and I made it to our counseling session on time. I picked her up from home and she was ready and excited about doing this with me. Smooth stayed home with children and handled everything while I was away. When I stepped into Mrs. Wilson's office, I became nervous and wasn't as prepared for this as I thought I was. My mother could tell, she told me that everything was going to be fine and that we could stop at any time.

"Hello Ciara and this must be your mother. Hello Ms. Robinson so glad to finally meet you. Did Ciara share with you that I was her counselor as well in the group home?" Mrs. Wilson asked.

"Hello I'm Brenda, Ciara's mother nice to meet you. Yes she told that you were her counselor, thank you for invited me here today." Brenda said.

"Great let's all have a seat. Now the reason way I asked Ciara to have you here because it is very important that we start from the beginning. I'm fully aware of the past and I believe that you also had a drinking problem as well Brenda. What I would like to do today is discuss the physiological drama that has effected Ciara and may play a big part in her life right now." Mrs. Wilson said.

"I had a bad drinking problem that stemmed from lack of affection. My husband had a gambling problem, he loved to gamble so much that it took a toll on me. He would spend more days and nights in the casinos, at the race track, or at the gambling house. Although he didn't cheat on me and have an affair with a woman, he had an affair with the love of his life, and that was gambling. I seek love and affection and found it with alcohol. It would help me sleep through the nights in an empty bed. It took the place of my husband. I had it under control and I was a functional drinker. I went to work and took care of home; but after my husband's death, I lost control and the drinking took over. I went from having a drink once a week to drinking every day. From drinking every day to drinking three times a day. Eventually, I lost my job and had to depend on public assistance. When I couldn't get a drink, I would take it out on Ciara, she was the only person close to me at the moment. All of my family had cut me off because of my drinking problem. That hurt me and once again I had no one to love me but the alcohol. For two years I was depressed and didn't know how to cope without alcohol. It would be days that I wouldn't eat but I had a drink. One time I forgot that Ciara was my daughter and called the police on her because I thought that I had an intruder in my home. The alcohol had taken over my life." Brenda cried.

Mrs. Wilson handed both me and her some Kleenex because I started to cry as well. I hugged my mother as she cried into the tissue. The room was quiet for a minute before I spoke and broke the silence.

"I still remember the day when you first hit me. I was sitting at the table doing my homework and I didn't understand a math problem so I asked you to help me. You came to the table to help me and your breath smelled like that you have been drinking. You became frustrated when I couldn't get the problem, smacked me, and made me go to my room. I didn't eat dinner that night because I was afraid to come back out of the room." I said.

"Ciara, do you feel that you drink because of lack of affection just like your mom?" asked Mrs. Wilson.

"Yes I feel that Eric's cheating ways has caused me to drink. The only thing different with me and my mother situation is that I don't hit or harm anyone. The alcohol helps me remain calm and makes me numb to all the bullshit, please excuse my language; that is going on around me. When Eric acts a fool, I take a drink. When I want to talk instead, I take a drink. When I feel like he's lying to me, I take a drink. I'm forcing myself to make it work and to keep my family together. I will never ever hit my children, I love them too much but I do hit Eric. He doesn't hit me back, but I feel good when I do and I'm afraid that one of these days that he would hit me back." I said.

"Brenda, is this your first time hearing any of this from Ciara? How is you and Ciara's relationship now?" Mrs. Wilson asked.

"This definitely my first time hearing all of this. Ciara and I are fine, I apologized for all the pain that I have caused in her life. After she was taken away from me, I got help and went through a rehabilitation program that helped me get over alcohol. It was hard in the beginning but during the program and that hard time I found God. A part of my life changed. I had to ask Ciara to forgive me. It's a blessing to be back in my daughter's life." Brenda said.

"I forgive my mother and we both are at a better place in our lives. She's a great grandmother and she's the only family that I have. When I was younger, I promised to never be the mother that she was and that I would never drink. I was so strong and I can't believe that I let the same disease that my mother had break me. Seeing my mother getting over alcoholism is proof that so can I. I can't do this alone and need her by my side. I know that Eric is my man but in all honesty he is the problem and the only counseling that Eric and I need is couple therapy. I will deal with that after I get help first for my drinking. Mrs. Wilson do you think that you can refer me to some AA meetings?"

"Yes Ciara I can do that. I will email you a list of AA meetings tomorrow. I'm so happy that we got a lot covered today. Thank you Brenda for coming, I'm happy that you overcame your illness. Ciara needs all your support and right now being a mother is very important." Mrs. Wilson said.

"I'm here for my daughter with any help that she needs. I can't and won't let her go down that same path as me." Brenda said.

"Great I'm looking forward to seeing you next week Ciara and Brenda feel free to join us if you like." Mrs. Wilson said walking us both to the door.

Once my mother and I made it back to my car in private, I wanted to thank her for coming. Today a lot of issues were revealed, that I know I wouldn't been able to say in front of Smooth.

"Thank you so much for coming with me today. You don't have to continue to come back with me if you don't want to." I said.

"Oh no I would come as long as you want and need me to. I'm here to support you always. You're my daughter and I love you." Brenda said.

"I love you too. Since Smooth has the children we can stay out. I was thinking that we could stop by the hospital to visit GG. Then after that we can grab a bite to eat."

My mother was fine with my plans. Before I pulled off, I called home to check on my family. From the sounds of things Smooth and the children were having a good time without me. We chatted about my mother and her new boyfriend on the way to the hospital. When we arrived, we checked in and found out that GG was no longer in ICU and had been stepped down to Telemetry. My mom and I got our visitor's passes and went to her room. Kelly was there alone with GG, they both were watching television.

"Hey Kelly. Hello GG, how are you doing?" I asked her giving her a big hug.

"Chile I'm fine, a little hungry. They got me on a strict diet and the food is horrible. Do you have something to eat in that big purse of yours?" GG said.

"Grandma, you can't be eating whatever you want to eat. That's why you're in the situation that you are in now." Kelly said. GG ignored her and started to pull the wires on her chest. "Please leave that alone because every time you pull one off, the nurse has to come back in here and put it back on," said Kelly.

"Why do I have to have all of this on my chest anyway?" GG asked.

"It's to keep track of your heart. They are monitoring your heart making sure that everything is fine. Please cooperate grandma. Remember once the test come back tomorrow and everything is fine the doctor will release you." Kelly said.

"It's good to see that you're better GG." Brenda said.

"Thanks Brenda, I'll feel even better once I get home." GG said sitting up in the bed.

She gave Kelly the side eye. I could tell that Kelly was getting on her last good nerve. GG didn't like anyone to tell her what to do. I asked Kelly to step out for a minute and we both excused ourselves. I could see that she needed a break as well. We went down to the hospital cafeteria.

"So what's going on with GG?" I asked.

"GG has diabetes and has known for a year." Kelly said.

"Are you serious? Why would she keep that away from you?" I asked.

"She said that she didn't want to tell Shawn or me because we would start to worry. She felt like she had everything under control but she doesn't. Her blood sugar was extremely high and caused her to collapse. After today I have to keep a track on everything that she eats." Kelly said.

"That's going to be the hard part because all of GG's food involves butter, grease, and lots of sugar." I said.

"I know and she's going to be pissed when she finds out that she can't drink her regular Coke and has to switch to the Diet Coke." Kelly said.

"It's definitely going to be a lifestyle change. If we all practice the same eating habits, it should be easier for her to do. Where is Shawn?"

"He's supposed to be on his way up here. He called me an hour ago, he needs to hurry up and get here. I love my grandmother and all but you know that you can't tell her nothing. She's starting to get on my nerves." Kelly said.

"I could see that all over your face. Me and my mother are going to grab a bite to eat after this, you should join us. It's going to be something quick and laid back. We both just came back from my counseling session.

"Girl I will go, I'm starving and craving tacos. Let's go to Fuego Loco,' said Kelly.

We talked for a bit and my phone went off alerting me that I had a text message. I read the message and it was from Kanye. My heart fluttered and I blushed like a school girl. I showed Kelly and she suggested that I text him back. I read the text message out loud, "*I miss u, can't stop thinking about u.*"

Kelly urged me to text him. "You know that you want to text him back so go head on and do so. I don't know why you fronting." She said laughing.

I miss u 2

Can I see u today?

I paused for a minute before I replied back. Apart of me wanted to see him badly. You know what I'm going to stop playing these games.

Yes

Great can't wait to see u

Kelly and I went back upstairs to the room. GG, my mother, and Shawn were all there. GG was eating a Chicken Caesar Salad that Shawn had bought her. Kelly looked at her eating the salad, then she looked back at Shawn. GG smiled happily as she ate her salad.

"What? Sis, it's a salad, isn't a salad consider to be healthy." Shawn said.

Kelly rolled her eyes. "Look now that you're finally here I'm leaving. Call me if anything happens or if you need me." Kelly told Shawn. She gave GG a hug and a kiss and told her to behave like a mother does their child. My mom and I told GG goodbye as well. Upon leaving the hospital when we got on the lower level we seen Vell. He was with a brown skinned girl. He didn't see us, Kelly and I wondered who the girl was and what were they doing up at the hospital. I thought that maybe she could be one of his relatives until the both of them kissed and he grabbed her booty. Kelly whispered to me so that my mother wouldn't hear her.

"Girl, Vell cheating on Aaliyah, or did they break up? You know I don't know what's going on because I don't fuck with the bitch."

"I didn't hear anything about the two of them breaking up. Last time I heard they were one big happy family." I said.

"Well we know that isn't true, I bet Niecy knows what's going on. We have to have a talk with her." Kelly said.

We all went to have tacos. It was tempting seeing all those margaritas pass me by. I really wish that I could have one. I was anxious and nervous to see Kanye. I dropped my mom off and went to meet him at our secret location. It was out of sight out of mind. When I arrived, he was already there waiting. He opened my car door and I stepped out wrapping my arms around him. We kissed deeply, "You have no idea how much I miss you," said Kanye. I looked deep into his eyes but quickly looked away. Kanye grabbed my chin and turned my face toward his. "What's wrong? You don't believe me?" He dropped to his knees with a box. I was shocked and told him to get up and stop playing.

"Are you crazy? I'm not going to marry you." I said.

"Will you be mines?" Kanye opened up the box and it was a necklace with a heart pendent.

"You play too much!" I said laughing.

Kanye laughed and got up from the ground putting the necklace around my neck. "When I saw this, I thought of you and had to buy it for you." He said.

"It's beautiful, thank you. I want you to know that I've been thinking about you like crazy." I said.

"When you ready to stop playing and start messing with a real man? Ciara, I could look at you and tell that you're not happy." Kanye said.

"I'm working on me right now and trying to fix myself. For some apparent reason I just can't stop seeing you. No matter how hard I try to cut you off. I think about you all the time; but if I'm going to be with you, I have to be officially done with him. I hope that you understand." I said.

"I understand, that's why I'm willing to wait on you. Sooner than later you two will be over soon."

My cell phone rang, it was Smooth calling me but I didn't answer.

"Whatever but anyway I have to go. I've been gone too long. I will call you when I can meet you again. Thank you for the necklace." I said walking back to get in my car.

Smooth was calling me again by now. Kanye had a pissed look on his face and I felt sorry that I had to leave like that. I answered my phone on the last ring.

"Hello Ciara, why do I have to keep calling your phone several times? What are you doing?" Smooth asked.

"I'm leaving my mother's house right now and on my way home. The first when you called I had to find my phone in my purse. What's up?" I said.

"Just checking on you. The children and I miss you, especially me." He said.

"I'm on my way now. I love you and be home soon."

After I ended my call, Kanye called me. I talked with him for a second and quickly got off the phone. I made it home safely but before I went in I put Kanye's number on the block list in fear that he might call back. I

146

went in the house and the children ran over to me quickly giving me hugs and kisses. Smooth was sitting on the couch watching baseball. I kissed him and sat next to him and he asked how my day was. I told him that it was great and shared everything that I did with the exception of going to see Kanye.

"I miss you baby, you've been gone all day. I hope you're ready to make it up to me tonight." Smooth said.

I hopped on his lap and straddled him smothering him with kisses. Erica and Eric Jr. laughed and climbed on him as well. Right then and there I realized how much family is very important. Smooth tickled me and the children, I fell out laughing on the couch. Smooth noticed the chain around my neck and touched it.

"This is nice, when did you get it?" Smooth asked.

"Oh this old thing, I've had it for a while. I just haven't worn it as much as my other jewelry." I lied and said.

Whoa! I dodged that bullet. I have to be more careful. I'm not good at cheating or juggling two men.

Chapter Ten

Smooth

I got up to leave the house early. The first stop I made was straight to my mother's house to check on her. I pulled into my mother's driveway and entered into her home with my key. When I walked in, the smell of bacon hit my nostrils. My mom was so busy cooking breakfast that she didn't even hear me come in. I startled her causing her to drop the spatula that she had in her hand.

"Boy don't you creep up on me like that!" My mother said hitting me.

"Sorry mom, how are you this morning?" I laughed asking her as I picked up the spatula from off the floor.

"I'm fine besides the fact that I'm still tired. Your baby girl kept me up late last night. For some apparent reason she didn't fall asleep till 12a.m. I'm not playing with her tonight, she's going to bed by 8p.m. Another thing you know that I had a very long talk Kayla. Eric you're treating her wrong. You could at least talk to her, that's the mother of your child."

"Ma, I got everything under control besides Kayla doesn't know how to talk to me. Don't let her fool you, she's disrespectful." I said.

"Well I hope that you get everything under control real soon because she will be home soon. Lawd knows I can't so she can take care of her child."

"Where is my baby girl at?" I asked.

"She's in there sleeping. Go ahead and wake her up so that she won't be up all night again."

I went in the room to wake her up. Variyah frowned up and started to cry. "Don't cry baby girl, your daddy is here." As soon as she heard my voice, she stopped crying and looked at me. She was spoiled already. I walked back in the kitchen and sat at the table. I ate breakfast with my mother and spent some time with both her and Variyah. My phone starting ringing and that only meant that is was time for me to handle my business. I kissed my mom and daughter, made sure they were cool and bounced. While I was out making my runs, Vell called telling me that Aaliyah fucked up his car. I laughed at his goofy ass for allowing her to do some bullshit like that. I told him that he needs to put her in check. I looked at the time and made my way to my destination. I owned a two flat building on the south side. The workers were laying the wood on the floors and doing the bathroom. I walked through the apartment checking to see what was finished and what needed to be done. I hired black workers instead of Mexicans, I was all for supporting black owned businesses. I have to admit they had the place looking great.

"Boss man how we looking?" I asked the older worker who was in charged.

"Eric, how are you? We are looking to be finished by next week. All we have to do next are the floors and paint. We went to go buy the paint today and getting started on that tomorrow. We are laying the carpet in the bedrooms too." He said.

"You got it looking good in here. We walked into the bedrooms making sure that everything was getting done as expected. It was a three bedroom unit. I checked out everything and stepped on the back porch. It was nice and sturdy. I felt assured that I would pass my inspection.

"The city will be here to inspect the property in twelve days. Do you think that you will be done by then?" I asked.

"Everything will be finished and you will pass inspection."

"Cool, are you hungry? Is it anything that you guys need?" I asked.

"Food!" One of the workers yelled from the front.

"I got you, does Popeyes sound good?" I asked.

They all said yes and I went to grab two buckets of chicken and some liters of pop for them to drink. I dropped everything off and I made a call to Aaliyah to find out what the hell was going on with her.

"What's up sis? Are you busy? I need to stop by and see you?" I said.

"Hey Smooth, I'm free just come over." Aaliyah said.

I drove to Aaliyah's place and when I got there she opened up the door smiling. I thought to myself this girl is crazy as hell. I bought us some chicken to eat as well. We sat down in the dining room eating and I got straight to the point.

"Sis, why did you fuck up Vell's car? What the hell is going on?" I asked her.

"Fuck Vell and his car, your friend knows exactly why I did it and I will do it all over again," said Aaliyah.

"You can't be out here acting crazy you have two daughters that you need to be concerned about. If something happens to you, who would take care of them?" I asked, being serious.

Aaliyah didn't want to hear what I was saying. She pulled out a cigarette and starting smoking. I don't know what the hell Vell did but whatever it was had changed her for the worst. She blew the smoke circles in the air.

"Smooth you're right, I let him get to me and that shit wasn't cool. What's done is done and I just need to move on with my life."

"Yes that's more like it. Allow him to be a father to his children and you be the mother that they need. Put that cigarette out, it isn't lady like." Aaliyah put out the cigarette and I continued talking. "Now that we talked about that I need you to do me a favor and go pick out some furniture for and things for your girl, Kayla. She will be out in two weeks and I need to have everything set up for her." I said.

"Cool what exactly am I buying? For how many rooms?"

"A living room, dining room, and bedroom set. A small kitchen table not anything too big and the basic things that you need for an apartment. Here is $10,000 that should work. I will text you the address that I need everything delivered to. When was the last time that you spoke with Kayla?" I asked.

"Cool that's enough to get everything that you need. I just spoke with Kayla two days ago. We talk all the time. When was the last time that you have spoken to her?" Aaliyah asked.

I laughed because I already know where this was heading and that Kayla had got in her ear as well. "Look I will talk to her once she is home." I said.

"Whatever you need to stop treating my friend like shit Smooth before you get fucked up too." Aaliyah said laughing.

"Yeah alright, I'm not Vell's crazy ass woman." I said.

Aaliyah laughed it off but I was serious as hell. I wish that Kayla would act a fool on me, she already knows what would happen if she got out of line. I gave Aaliyah the money for the furniture and got out of there. As I drove off, I called Vell to tell him that I just left his baby mama's house and had a talk with her. I'm not going to lie what my buddy is doing is foul but who am I to judge with the shit I'm out here doing. This was the first and last time that I will get in his business. I had my hands full already with my situation and had to be concerned and prepared for Ciara when she found out about Variyah. I called my queen to see what she was doing. Ciara only spoke with me for five minutes because she was busy at the boutique. Maybe I will slide up there and surprise her for lunch one of these days. Really I didn't have shit else to do so I slid over to Ant's crib. Ant and Kelly was in the house chilling and smoking when I showed up.

"I swear you two are made for one another." I said having a seat on the sectional.

"Smooth, you want to hit the blunt playa?" Ant asked me.

I declined. "No I'm cool. What's up Kelly? How is GG doing?"

"Hey Smooth, GG is doing better. She's back at home being stubborn you know that she doesn't like anyone telling her what to do," said Kelly.

Ant was ready to play a new game that his mother had bought him. He hooked the game up and we played a few rounds. Kelly went to her room leaving us alone. His phone rang and it was Vell calling him crying like a bitch telling him how Aaliyah fucked up his car and that he needed Kelly to get him a rental until his car was out of the shop.

"You have to ask Kelly if she would get the rental for you. Hold on let me tell her to come here." Ant said to Vell on the phone.

He yelled Kelly's name and she came running down the stairs. "What's up bae?" She asked.

"Here Vell wants to ask you something." Ant said passing Kelly his cell phone.

Kelly listened to Vell talk and she agreed to rent him a car. She passed Ant the phone and went to go get dressed. Ant talked to Vell for a minute and got off the phone because he was losing against me in the game. Ten minutes later Kelly left the house and we were alone to talk. I talked about what was really bothering me.

"Man, Kayla got my mother thinking that I'm treating her bad. She had a talk with my mom's and told her all types of crazy shit. My mother in my ear saying, Smooth stop treating her so wrong; she don't know the real Kayla man." I said.

"Between you and Vell, I don't know who has the biggest problem on their hands. What you going to do when Kayla get out? You know that she isn't going to remain calm and keep quiet. Kayla was crazy when you met her, but yet and still you decided to pop her crazy ass off. Smooth, you fucked up this time playa and I'm just keeping it one hundred with you," said Ant.

"I know but it's not going to happen anymore. I'm a changed man now and only want to be with Ciara. I will forever take care and love my daughter; but as far as Kayla ain't no love there. I mean I don't hate her and I appreciate everything that she did for me."

"I believe that you can change, hell I did and look at Kelly and me. It's peaceful just having one and only one, especially after all that crazy shit that I went through with Ebony's whore ass. Red has even calmed down and stopped having multiple hoes and settled with Niecy. It's too much shit going on out here, you can't trust these hoes." Ant said.

"Speaking of Red where the hell has he been?" I asked

"Red at home trying to make a baby." Ant laughed and said.

We were both laughed making fun of Red that he called my phone. When I answered the phone, we were in the middle of laughing and Red asked what we were laughing about. "We laughing at you man. Where the hell you been at? Ant said that you were in the house trying to make a baby." I said laughing.

"Man fuck the both of you, I'm on my way over there," said Red.

An hour later he arrived and we all kicking it. Red used to the biggest player of us all back then. He was known as the man to trick off and blow all his money on strippers. We were all amazed when he settled down with Neicy, I mean don't get me wrong she's nice and physically his type. Neicy was a college graduated not just the average girl that he dated in the past that didn't have a high school diploma or GED. We all could see that our buddy had changed and we weren't mad more like surprised.

"Red, I thought it wasn't a woman in the world that could change you. Remember how you went to the strip club every day and sponsored a different stripper every week," Ant said laughing.

"I know man I went from throwing money on strippers to only spending it on Neicy. Honestly I think that she's the one. She got a nigga opened I'm not going to lie. The only problem is that she has a problem with get pregnant. We've been trying and you all know how I don't have problems with making babies. I guess this payback for all the abortions that I paid for in my past." Red said sipping on his drink.

"Smooth doesn't have any problems making babies either." Ant said laughing.

"Fuck you Ant and pay me my damn money. I beat your ass three times get them dollars together." I said.

Red, Ant, and I kicked it until Kelly returned home. She got the rental car for Vell and put us all out. Ant paid me my money and Red left to go home to his girl. Before I went in I checked on my blocks to make sure that everything was running smoothly. All my workers were straight and the count was right. After I left I drove home riding down Washington Blvd. and I could see that someone was following me. I grabbed my piece and was ready to blast any fuck nigga that tried to pull it. I made a left onto Hamlin Ave. and the black van was still following me from a distance. Once I made it to Congress I made a right and jumped on the Eisenhower and the black van kept straight ahead. The driver had on a mask and was on some bullshit tonight and ready to die. I got on the line and notify everyone about the black van. I called an emergency meeting and told everyone to meet me at the spot. Twenty minutes later everyone showed up and we discussed that I was a target but we had to find out who was after me and why. Living in Chicago you had to always watch your front and your back because any day you could meet your maker. It was a grimy city where niggas didn't want to earn shit but instead take yours. I made sure that my people were on the job trying to find out everything about the black van. My phone rang and the caller on the other line told me that they found the black van empty on the north side in Rogers Park. Inside the van they found nothing, the van was cleaned and someone dumped it there. I didn't know who was behind everything but I was going to find out. It was going to be them instead of me and I had to lay there ass out first.

Chapter Eleven

Aaliyah

It was 9:00 a.m. and I was still in my bed. The twins were over my Aunt's house spending time with her. My Auntie was giving me a break and I sure and the hell needed it. The house was quiet and peaceful. I just laid in my bed and stared up at the ceiling thinking about everything. My money was getting tight and after the many episodes of me acting crazy Vell refused to give me any money to help me out. I fucking hated him, I wish that he would just die so that I could collect my insurance policy and move on with my life. I know that I said that I was going to stop acting crazy and shit but I lied. I'm going to make Vell's life a living nightmare and plus the bitch who he decides to be with. What's crazy is that I still don't know who Vell was having sex with the day that I caught him. I tried to call AT&T to retrieve his phone records but they wouldn't give it me. He has my number on the block list because of the many times that I've tried to get into his voicemail several times. That's why I took advantage of fucking up his car last week. I put sugar in his tank and busted all the windows out of it. I wanted to key it but I didn't have time because the police was coming. The tears rolled down my face as I started to cry. My phone started ringing and I really didn't feel like talking to anyone right now. It was Kayla so I answered because I needed to talk to her anyway.

"Hello, what's up Aaliyah boo? Nine more days and I will be free!" Kayla said happily into the phone. She quickly turned her happiness down when she heard me crying and sniffing into the phone. "Friend what happen?!

Vell bet not had put his hands on you because I will go crazy on his ass!" Kayla said.

"I'm so depressed and if I don't get a job soon I will be broke. Vell's hoe ass not answering for me anymore or giving me any money. My whole world is crashing Kayla." I cried.

"Please don't tell me that you spent all that money that he left in the house that fast. How much do you have left?" Kayla asked.

"I only have $6000 left and I'm going to run through that in a month. I have the mortgage, utilities to pay, and have to buy food." I said.

"You better stretch that cash girl. Don't worry I will be out soon and I will be connecting with my girl Cherish once I get out. If you want to be down you can too," said Kayla.

"Girl I would do anything to make some money right now. I hate being broke, hell I almost sold a few of my bags and shoes." I said.

"It ain't that bad besides Vell will never have you out there like that. I can't see him letting you and his daughters starve or be homeless. No matter how much he dislikes you, he will never let that happen."

"Girl I fucked up his car and now he's upset with me and not answering his phone. I guess he said fuck me and the twins." I said.

"Aaliyah I thought you said that you were going to stop acting crazy and just move on. Hell when you do shit like that you're taking money out of your family mouth. Now, he has to spend that money on his car."

"You know when you're mad at someone and you can't get to them but you see their car, your first reaction is to take it out on their car. All remember is swinging that bat." I said.

"Wow I wasn't prepared to hear all of this. Have you spoke to Smooth?" Kayla asked.

"As a matter of fact, I did. He came by here last week and gave me $10,000 to go shopping for your place. I haven't been yet because I was waiting on you to call so I can ask you what you prefer."

"He did, my baby daddy is so sweet. I want all white everything all through my house in every room. I like yellow too, you can add that color in as well," said Kayla.

"Okay I got you and going to hook you up friend. I told him that he better stop being mean to you too." I said.

"Girl don't worry I got a trick for his ass friend. See Smooth thinks that he can still control me but he has another thing coming. I've changed and I'm ready to see my baby girl and never let her go." Kayla said.

"I feel you it's all about the children at the end. I'm seriously going to stop all my craziness and get my life together." I said.

"I hope so because once I get out we're going to be on our money. Like Lil Kim say, 'Fuck Niggas Get Money'. That's the motto friend. I have to go now. I love you and see you when I get out," said Kayla.

"Love you too friend, see you soon." I said and ended the call.

Kayla snapped me back into reality so I got up and jumped in the shower. It was going to be 80 degrees today so I put on my coral and white stripe maxi dress, coral sandals, and sunhat. I curled my hair really pretty and sprayed my body with Very Sexy perfume, it was my favorite. Before I stepped out I made sure that I was on point. I looked good and I was ready for the day. I left out of the house and my next door neighbor was sitting on her porch. She looked at me up and down as I walked to my car. I looked back at the bitch and she rolled her eyes. I swear one of these days I was going to beat her ass but not today, I was too pretty to be fighting and in a good mood. I pulled off blasting Lil Kim and Junior Mafia and sang, 'Fuck niggas get money' as I drove down the street. I pulled up to Ashley's Furniture to buy Kayla's things. When I walked inside, I noticed a white salesman and black saleswoman on the floor. I walked over to the woman and asked for her help because today I was spending money and I know that they get paid off commission.

"Hello are you looking for anything in particular that I could help you with today?" The saleswoman asked.

"Hello and yes I am. I would like to see what you have in white. I'm looking for a white sectional, dining room set, and bedroom set." I said.

"Great! I can help you, please follow me."

One hour later I picked out everything that I needed. I called Smooth to get the address and set delivery up for

160

next week. The saleswoman was happy because I had spent close to $6000 in the store. After that I went to Bed Bath &Beyond to pick out some small appliances. For a pop of color, I picked out yellow. I bought a toaster, toaster oven, can opener, coffee maker, and etc. I also hooked up her bedroom in yellow, white, and grey. My phone started vibrating and it was Niecy calling me.

"What's up stranger? Where the hell have you been?" I asked her answering my phone on the first ring.

"Hey girl sorry about being MIA but I've been busy. What are you doing today?" Niecy asked.

"Nothing much. I'm out making runs right now. Why, what's up?" I asked.

"Today I'm having a small barbecue and I would love if you would come."

"Cool. I will slide over there later today. Do I need to bring anything?" I asked.

"No just bring yourself and see you later." Niecy said.

"See you later boo." I said and ended the call.

The Barbecue

I arrived at the barbecue a quarter after five. As soon as I got there, I walked over to Niecy to let her know that I made it. She was busy arguing with Red about something and didn't pay much attention so I helped myself to a sit. Niecy had table and chairs set up, I sat at an empty table alone. I scrolled through my phone making on the internet surfing various sites. Ciara and Kelly were there sitting at another table. Kelly looked over at me whispering to Ciara, I swear Kelly could be so fucking childish that's why I can't stand her ass. I knew that she was talking about me because everyone at the table looked over at me. I didn't pay them any mind and moments later two other girls sat at the table with me. Niecy made her way over to my table to speak.

"Hey Aaliyah thank you for coming." She said giving me a hug.

"Hey what's up, you know that I come to everything that you have." I said.

"The food is in the kitchen." Niecy said to all of us who sitting at the table.

I got up and walked passed the table where Kelly and everyone was sitting at and she laughed when I walked by. "Be cool, Aaliyah, just be cool," I said to myself inside my head. I fixed my plate and noticed that all the fellas were in the house. I was looking to see if Vell was here but he wasn't. I spoke to everyone and went back outside to have a seat. When I walked passed them again, Kelly laughed again, this time I didn't ignore her.

"You are so immature, grow up." I said

"Who are you talking too?" Kelly asked with an attitude.

"I'm talking to you and whoever else that's laughing." I said.

Kelly got loud and jumped out of her chair. "Aaliyah go over there and have a seat before I beat your ass!"

"Make me have a seat, Bitch!" I said.

Ant, Smooth, and Red ran outside. Ant pulled her back and they both went inside. Everyone calmed down and resumed what they were doing. I walked back to have a seat and ate my food. Niecy and Red came over and asked if I was cool.

"You good Aaliyah?" Red asked.

"I'm good." I said.

He walked off leaving me and Niecy alone. "Aaliyah if you feel uncomfortable you don't have to be here." She said.

"I'm very comfortable she's the one who isn't. I'm so tired of Kelly always fucking with me. She better be cool because I'm not for the bullshit. Period!" I said.

"I will talk with her but the last thing I want to do is make you feel uncomfortable," said Niecy.

"Girl, I'm cool don't worry about me." I said.

Someone called Niecy to come over and she excused herself to go see what they wanted. I continued to eat my food and I looked and my face dropped. Vell had arrived and he looked really nice. He looked over at me and walked inside the house. I wanted to get out of there not because I was afraid, I wanted to leave because we weren't there together and I really didn't want everyone to know that we were separated. When he came back outside, he came over to the table and had a seat right beside me.

"Are you cool? Even though we into it, I'm not going to let shit happen to you," said Vell.

"I'm cool." I said very short and fast.

"Why you fuck up my car like that Aaliyah?" Vell aksed.

"If you looking for an apology, you're not going to get it." I said.

"Where are the twins?"

"You are concerned about your daughters now? You wasn't concerned about them while you were out fucking another bitch." I smiled and said.

"Aaliyah, I will always be concerned about them 24/7." He said.

"Well since you're so concerned, I need some money so that I can buy some food."

"Ain't no money, your ass better go and get some food stamps. What you think you're too good for that?" Vell said.

Before I acted a fool at this barbecue and smacked the shit out of Vell, I decided to leave. I didn't want to ruin everything at Niecy's place and embarrass myself. I waved goodbye to Niecy and left out the same way that I came in. By the time that I made it to my car, Vell ran up behind me and grabbed my arm. I looked at his hands, "If you don't get your mutherfucking hands off me, I will cut them off!" I said.

Vell removed his hands holding both of them in the air. "I don't want to get cut again. Look I didn't mean what

I said. I will never let you or my girls starve. I will swing by there tomorrow to drop off some money." He said.

"Whatever, just call before you show up at my place. By the way the mortgage needs to be paid as well. I know you don't want us to be homeless neither." I said.

"Aaliyah, I will pay it but you need to get a job. Ain't shit wrong with you." Vell said.

"Don't tell me what I need to do when you not doing what you're supposed to be doing. That was being faithful to me and being and home for the twins. I've been there since the beginning and by your side. These hoes don't give a fuck about you. They will cry and fall out at your funeral and go home to fuck another man. I was honest, real, and down for you. So please don't tell me what to do because I did my mutherfucking job 24/7, no days off!" I said.

Vell stood there looking silly as I got in my car and drove off. How dare he talk down on me like I didn't do shit for him. He got me fucked up but I know one thing for sure is that I'm no longer going to let him upset me. He think I'm a joke but I will have the last laugh. I'm ready to fire off on all them from Vell, to Kelly, and anyone else who wants to get it. I'm not worried about Miss Ciara because my girl Kayla is going to take care of her ass. I've had enough of Kelly's little tough ass, she swear that she can beat the world. I don't know how Ant could even deal with her, let alone marry her, she's so damn immature.

Meanwhile Back At the Barbecue

"Vell, what did you do to make Aaliyah leave? I hope that you didn't make her go home." Niecy said.

"That damn girl is crazy and no I didn't make her leave. She made her own decision to do that. I was conversing with her and she started talking slick. I made sure that she was cool after her and Kelly altercation," said Vell.

Niecy and Vell were in the kitchen talking. Kelly came inside interrupting them. "Vell, I almost had to beat your baby mama's ass. She's so lucky that everyone held me back because I was about to tag that ass. I don't know how you deal with her, she's so damn irritating." Kelly said.

"Excuse me Kelly, can I talk to you alone?" Niecy asked.

"Sure what's up girl?" Kelly asked as they both walked into Niecy's bedroom.

"Kelly, I'm going to ask you something and I hope that you don't get upset. Why do you always pick on Aaliyah? I mean, I know that you don't like her, that's your choice and I totally get that. But why do you always have to provoke her to fight you? Why not say nothing to her at all? Every time you two are around one another it's a problem," said Niecy.

"Niecy, I understand that she's your friend but that bitch is fake. Every time I see her she makes me want to punch her in the face. It's a free world and I can say whatever I want to say."

"See that is so damn immature of you, it's like you're bullying her. That's not cool and I just can't sit back and let it happen. The next time that I have an event I would like if you can control your actions. I consider you a friend and I consider Aaliyah a friend as well. I don't know about all this fakeness that you're speaking of because she's never been fake to me," said Niecy.

"You know what Niecy I won't bother to come to another one of your events if she is going to be there because if she says anything to me I'm not going to control my actions." Kelly said.

"Kelly it's not that serious and now you making me choose. All I'm saying is today, what I seen, wasn't cool. You have no idea what she's going through right now. If you can't be in the same room with someone that you don't like then you have a lot more growing up to do. In the real world you're not going to get along with everyone and you're going to have to bite your tongue." Niecy said.

Niccy heard Red call her name and left Kelly standing in the room alone. Kelly couldn't believe that someone had talked to her like that. For the first time she wasn't upset and thought about what Niecy had said. Kelly was aware what was going on with Aaliyah because of the day that she got the rental car for Vell. Kelly picked Vell up from Victoria's place, he left out the back door instead of the front door. Although she didn't like Aaliyah, she told Vell that he was foul for fucking with the girl that lived right next door to them. He told her not to tell anyone so she never told Ciara but she did speak to Ant about it. Ant told her to stay out of it and to mind her business because Aaliyah doesn't know. Vell told Kelly that his girlfriend Victoria had gotten pregnant and had a miscarriage. That explained why she and Ciara had seen them both at Cook County Hospital when they were leaving. Kelly went back outside and enjoyed the rest of Niecy's barbecue, she didn't tell anyone about her and Niecy's conversation.

Chapter Twelve

Denise

The barbecue was finally over and I was so happy. Red, Smooth, Ant, and Vell were all outside cleaning up. I was in the house straighten things out and cleaning up as well. Ciara and Kelly offered to stay and help but I told them that I was fine and thanked them for coming. I was done washing my last pot out that had the greens in it. All the fellas came inside and said good bye and thanked me for inviting them. Vell pulled me to the side and asked if he could talk to me and I didn't mind that.

"Niecy I know that Aaliyah and you are friends and I want to ask you if you can drop this money off to her tomorrow?" He asked.

"Sure no problem, I can do that. Why didn't you just give it to her in the first place?" I asked him.

"At first I didn't want to give her nothing because that's what she's used to me doing all the time. Plus I'm still mad about her fucking up my car." Vell said.

He counted out the money and gave it to me. I promise to give Aaliyah the money and put it inside my purse. Everyone was finally gone and Red and I was home alone. Red sat down on the couch and I poured me and him a glass of Hennessy on the rocks. I'm not a drinker but after today I deserved a drink. Red laughed at me as I passed him his drink.

"What are you laughing at Mr.?" I asked him laughing.*

"At you with that glass in your hand. You need you a drink to unwind after everything today." He said.

"Red your friends are something else but I love them. Every time I get all of them together it's like being caught in the middle of a battle. I'm like the peacemaker of the group and trying to make everyone friends. For now on I'm done with the peacemaking shit." I sipped my drink.

"That's your best bet because Kelly and Aaliyah will never get along baby. I don't know why they don't because that's women business. From the first day they met they just didn't click."

"Kelly keeps saying that Aaliyah is fake but I don't see it. That still doesn't give you a reason to always want to fight every time that you see one another. Whatever happened to women acting like women? I just don't get down with all that fighting." I said.

"Kelly is street and hood but not in a bad way. All her life she had to fight and prove herself because she's small. She didn't have a mother to teach her how to be a lady. Both of her parents went to jail. Her grandmother tried her best to raise her. Now you on the other hand was raised by both of your parents. They taught and prepared you for life. You're quiet and reserved yet when it's time for you to go off you do it respectfully. That's what attracted me to you. Niecy you are different from all the women that I've dated. I didn't have to save you or tell you want to do or how to act. A lot of men could be intimidated by you but I wasn't. I love that shit, I love you girl. You're my Beyoncé." Red said.

"I love you too and you're my Jay Z." We both laughed and clicked our glasses together.

"Seriously I'm going to marry you, buy you a big house, and you're going to have my babies," said Red.

I was happy and sad at the same time because I knew that I had a problem with getting pregnant. My eyes watered and Red jumped up to hold me and ask me what was wrong. "Red I want a big family, you know four children but you and I both know that it's impossible." I cried.

"Baby why do you feel that way? We are going to do whatever it takes for you to have children. Don't be so negative, you're going to have my babies." He said kissing me.

I kissed him back and we both put down our glasses and continued to kiss passionately. Red laid me down on the couch and kissed my neck. It turned me on making me want him. He pulled my dress over my head and pulled out his dick. He kissed me as he entered inside me and pumped his dick deep inside me. I moaned, "I love you so much Red." In his ear as his strokes speeding up. Fifteen minutes later Red was finished and told me that he love me too. We still wasn't done and had round two in the shower and round three in the bed. I fell asleep on top of Red's chest.

The next day we had morning sex and went to have breakfast at Epple's Restaurant. I had a broccoli, ham, and cheddar omelet Red had steak, grits, and eggs. He ate everything like he always does. My man could eat but he kept himself up by working out. He wasn't buff but he had muscle. Just the right amount. I don't really care for a buff man but what he lacked he made up for. Red had an anaconda, a big dick. That's why in his past he had all the women chasing after his ass and going crazy. What I liked about him was that he didn't brag about it. I remember the first time that he pulled it out, I was like that isn't going in me. I was scared and it took me a while to get used to it. Now I take his dick like a pro. We wrapped things up and Red took me home and left back out to handle business. It was still early and I wanted to lie down a bit before going out. To be honest after yesterday, I was still tired from throwing my barbecue. I wrapped my hair up, put my scarf on, and threw on a tank top and some cute girly boxer shorts. I turned down the central air just a little bit, it was close to 90 degrees out but inside here it was 30 degrees. My lips were dry so I looked in my purse for my lip-gloss. That's when I noticed that the money Vell gave to me to give to Aaliyah. Damn I didn't feel like going outside and I know that she needed this money. I called her to see if she would come by here instead to pick it up.

"Hey Niecy." Aaliyah said sounding all dry into the phone.

"Damn hello to you too. Don't sound too happy to hear from me." I said

"Girl, I'm still upset about everything that happened yesterday at your barbecue," said Aaliyah.

"Well I'm sorry to hear that and trust me I wasn't happy either but hey today is a new day. Forget about that right now I called to tell you that Vell left some money for you. I was suppose to drop it off to you but Aaliyah I'm too tired to move. Can you please come by to pick it up?" I said.

"Yes I will be there, just give me an hour." She said.

"Okay bye, see you in an hour."

Two hours later Aaliyah called my phone. I had dozed off and missed two calls from Red so I called him back. I buzzed the door for and went to the washroom to freshen up. Aaliyah and I sat in the kitchen. I offered her something to drink as I went in the fridge to grab a bottle of water. I gave Aaliyah one and her money that Vell had left her.

"Thank you friend, I appreciate it." She said happily.

"Oh now you're happy, because earlier you didn't sound like it." I said.

"Never mind me that was earlier and I apologize. Now that I have some money I can buy some food. I'm so happy that my girls are over my aunt's house because I didn't have any food to feed them for the week." Aaliyah said.

"Why didn't you tell me that? I could've gave you the money. Don't ever think that you can't ask me for nothing. Anything that you and the twins need just let me know." I said getting upset

"I know I have a lot of people who are willing to help me but I could never ask for help. Besides Vell has the money to take care of us." She said.

"I understand that but that's Vell money and what if something happens to him? What are you going to do? Have you ever thought about going back school?"

"That's why I have an insurance policy on him. If anything happens to him, the twins and I are straight."

"Girl you sound so silly because if that man goes to jail right now all you have left is that $700 that he just left you. All the money that he has is counted for a lawyer and commissary. You can kiss that goodbye. Anyway what is it that you like to do? What is your dream job?" I asked her.

"First off he's not going to jail so don't jinx us like that. Let me knock on wood," said Aaliyah. I rolled my eyes at her simple ass. I was one second from throwing her ass out of my house. Aaliyah looked at me and changed her tone. "I always wanted to be an interior decorator."

"That's a good field and why you're sitting in the house all day you need to do some research on that field."

"I could do that but in the meantime I have to survive. Vell will have to do a better job and take care of us. Do you know that he told me to get on public assistance?" Aaliyah said.

"Well if you have to get food stamps that's your business. Better that than not having any food at all. If you feel like you to go to take a hand out, then you need to be working because if you don't make your own money, a hand out is what you will always need." I said.

Aaliyah rolled her eyes and wasn't trying to hear nothing what I was saying. We talked about everything that happened yesterday at my barbecue. I didn't tell her that I had talked with Kelly because she would've ask me what we talked about and I didn't have time for all of that. After Aaliyah finally left, I called my man to check on him. We talked for thirty minutes, I was trying to get him to drop me off some food but he was too far away. I heated up some barbecue that we had from yesterday. It was Sunday and I was bored out of my mind. I really couldn't get into too much because I had to go to work in the morning. My bored ass decided to watch television so I found a Lifetime Movie on Demand to watch. The movie was okay but I just really wanted to go somewhere. I called Ciara but she didn't answer after that I called Kelly and she did answer.

"Hey Niecy what's up?" Kelly asked.

"Girl nothing I'm bored, what are you doing?"

"I'm not doing anything but sitting over GG's house, you should come over and sit with us for a few hours." I said.

"Okay I will be over there soon."

It was 4 p.m. so I threw on a short outfit and some sandals. I called Red to tell him where I was going. It took me almost an hour to make it to GG's house because it was so much traffic. Everyone was outside trying to enjoy the weather. Kelly and GG was in the house chilling under the air conditioner. Although it was hot outside GG cooked her Sunday dinner. I washed my hands and made myself a plate, I was starving.

"GG this food is so good. Can you please teach me how to cook?" I asked.

"Sure babe whenever you're ready just let me know," said GG.

"I will be ready as soon as it cools down, like in the fall. That way I could be prepared for the holidays." I said.

"Okay chile. Let me go and lie down and watch some television until I fall asleep." GG left us alone.

Kelly washed my plate out that I used. "Where is Ciara? I called her early but she didn't answer." I asked Kelly.

"I talked to Ciara earlier for five minutes. Ciara usually spends her Sunday with her family. She calls it 'Family Day.'"

"That's cool, I can't wait till I have my children and we can have 'Family Day.'"

"Me too I plan on having two children. How many do you want?" Kelly asked me.

"I want three, God willing if he bless me. I have a hard time getting pregnant." I said.

GG walked back in the kitchen and went in the refrigerator. She tried to cut herself another slice of cake, a really big slice of cake. Kelly cut the slice in half and gave it to her. "Niecy just pray about it and give it to God. All things are possible through him. Never say never and never give up or lose faith. God will bless you with a house full of children. Pray for a good husband too, it's shortage on those." GG said and went back in her room.

Kelly brought up our conversation about yesterday and apologized to me. "Niecy whenever you have an event I will come rather or not if Aaliyah is there. It would be silly of me not to, I'm sorry for putting you in that position in the first place." She said.

"No problem I know that you didn't mean it. You and I were both upset at the time and when people are upset they say things that they really don't mean. I just want everyone to put their differences to the side and have a good time." I said.

"I understand besides I have other things to be concerned about and GG is my top priority. I don't have time for the bullshit, I will just go crazy if I lose her," said Kelly.

Kelly began to cry and I hugged her. I didn't like that she was hurting because I started crying too. We both prayed together and asked God to watch over GG.

Later on that night while Red was in the shower, I went through his pants pocket but didn't find anything. Yes I go through my man things, hell he was gone the whole day. Ain't no telling what Red was out there doing. I got up and went in the closet and checked the shopping bags. He went to the mall today without me. He had a Gucci bag, Macy's bag, and a bag from Zales. My eyes lit up when I saw the small box. I could hear Red getting out of the shower so I hurried up and ran back in bed. Red stepped up smelling fresh with a towel wrapped around his waist. I decided to ask him what he bought while he was out.

"Hey Mr. How was your day? I see that you went to the mall. Did you buy me anything?" I asked.

"I did a little shopping and picked up a few things." Red said. I massaged his shoulders and back, I can see that he isn't going to tell me. Damn! I want to know what's in the small box but I don't want to spoil the surprise.

Chapter Thirteen

Tia

Tommy and I haven't been seeing eye-to-eye ever since our fight. Our household has been tarnished because of his cheating ways. It's funny how one day were happily celebrating my birthday and engagement. Then the day after it's back to being unhappy. I was so busy filming my 'Tia Teach Me How Too Strip' videos that I didn't even care when Tommy came and gone. Tommy still came home at night, he knew better because if he didn't his shit was going to be out on the front lawn. At night we still slept in the same bed but he wasn't getting no pussy. I will wrestle with him every night to keep him off of me. I wasn't playing with him and stood on not having sex with him. Besides every time that I looked at the picture of him in the grocery store with another woman made me sick to my stomach. That was some personal shit to do with someone, you just don't grocery shop with any random bitch. I hate that my friend couldn't get a picture of the woman's face. It was obvious why Tommy was with her because she had a nice shape. I'm not going to lie she was thicker than me and Tommy is a sucker for a big booty. My feelings was hurt that he lied about it and you can see him on the picture very clearly. Pictures don't lie, they told every thing and what I seen was my man cheating on me with another female. I didn't even bother to tell my sister's what was going. My mother could tell that something wasn't right but she didn't get involved. All she wanted was one of her daughters to get married and give her some grandbabies. I had plans to do all that but I can't fake it. If I'm not happy, I work on what's making me unhappy but if it doesn't want to change then I have no other choice than to let it go. I thought about Ciara and every thing that her and Smooth has been through. I picked up my cellphone and decided to call her.

Ring! Ring! Ring! "Hello what's up Tia, I was just thinking about calling you but you beat me to it," said Ciara.

I sniffed and the next thing you know I started crying.

"Tia what's wrong? What is going on? Where is Tommy?" Ciara asked hysterically.

"Ciara it's all over Tommy is cheating with a female who is thicker than me and possibly even prettier. My friend caught them together grocery shopping and took a picture of them both. She sent it to me and I confronted Tommy about it but of course he lied and said that it wasn't him. I called off our engagement and threw his ring back at him." I said crying into the phone.

"Girl wait a minute, are you serious? First thing you need to do is get your ring back, don't ever give back your ring. Always keep your ring and wear it at all times because the minute that you take it off people start speculating and being in your business. Second, stop crying I know that you're hurt about finding and a seeing that the female is thicker. Let me tell you something Tia it's always going to be someone prettier, thicker, and younger. Third, keep on being the good woman that you are. Don't stop being yourself and if you continue to have sex with him make his ass wear a condom. You don't know if he's wearing one with her or not so protect yourself."

"I hate that I didn't see the female's face. My friend only got a side glimpse of her. I mean it hurt me to my heart when I seen the picture of him in the grocery store with another woman. You can tell that their relationship is fresh because Tommy used to go grocery shopping with me in the beginning." I said.

"Tia ain't no telling how long they have been talking. You can tell that Tommy and Smooth are cousins. They both are professional cheaters and good at it. At least he doesn't have a baby on you and a crazy baby momma in hiding." Ciara said.

"Ciara, I don't know how you do it. If I find out that Tommy does have any muther fucking children out there I'm killing his ass. That child is going to be a bastard fucking around with me. I'm serious as hell, see now I'm getting worked up again and ready to fight. I feel like riding around and looking for his ass!" I said.

"Tia don't go looking for him you just continue doing you and if you find out anything else then you strike. I hate that you're going through this and hurt because I know how it feels. Going through it with Smooth he had me thinking that I was the problem and not good enough for him. I had to realize that it wasn't me and stop beating myself up inside. These men will drain you of your joy if you let them." Ciara said.

Ciara and I continued to talk about our trifling ass men. She was on point about a lot of things, the best advice comes from a person who has been through it. That was the reason why I asked and confided in her. I was comfortable with telling her that I feel insecure about my body once that I saw Tommy with that thick ass girl. I wouldn't let him ever know about that. Men at times like to throw things back in your face. She had me wanting to get butt injections. I was furious and envious that she had my man's attention. I wonder if she know about me. These chicks today don't care about being the side chick. She just don't know that I fight for what's mine and will kill a bitch. I hated that I was feeling this way because right now I should be the happiest woman in the world. My career is rising, I make my own money, and last but not least I'm a boss. Ciara is right I can't allow this situation to still my joy. If Tommy is going to be with me that's fine. If he's not that's great too because at the end of the day I can't make a man stay where he doesn't want to be.

I called Tommy's phone and he answered right away. This time I didn't yell or curse him out, instead I remained calm. Tommy was shocked and told me that he would be home soon. I simply said okay and I will have dinner ready. I cooked his favorite dish and slipped into some sexy lingerie. I went in the safe and put on my engagement ring. I wasn't going to let the next woman take my man, I was running this. So what she was a thicker than me, I had his heart. I'm going to make sure that he stops running around with this one. I was going to play Tommy's little game and beat him at it.

Meanwhile

Tommy and Ebony were laying up at his trap house. Ebony was naked and busy sucking on his dick while he counted his money. She swallowed him up and after she was done she poured herself another glass of wine. Tommy got up and started putting on his clothes.

"Why do we have to go? I don't want this to end." Ebony whined and said.

Tommy ignored her and put on his shoes. Ebony caught on and began to get dress. She threw on her dress and heels, she didn't have on any underwear because Tommy preferred that she didn't wear any. He smacked Ebony on her luscious ass. Her drunk ass twerked for him, shaking her ass in his face.

"Shake that ass for daddy!" Tommy said.

"Anything for daddy, whatever daddy wants, daddy gets," said Ebony.

Tommy put all the money in the duffle bag and Ebony's grimy ass watched his every move. What Tommy didn't know was that Ebony was now plotting to stick him up. She told her cousin Rio about how she met a nigga down in Texas who had plenty of cash and how easy it was to get his ass. Rio was all up for it because he didn't have any money. Rio sold marijuana and it wasn't really much money in that. Rio was also planning to stick Smooth up as well, he was the one that was following him. Ebony wasn't aware of him plotting to get Smooth. Ebony was in a trance and didn't hear Tommy call her name.

"Renee do you hear me calling you!"

Ebony was high off the ecstasy pill that she popped earlier. "I don't want to go yet." She said and pulled her dress back off and started twerking and dancing naked in front of Tommy.

Tommy became pissed off and snatched her ass up. "Look you better stop playing with me and put your fucking dress back on. When I say it's time to go, it's time to go. Shit I got to get home and you acting stupid and shit!"

"I'm sorry daddy, I just wanted to have some fun. You never have any fun with me anymore. All we do is come to the trap house and fuck," said Ebony.

"Renee, I told you my situation, don't start tripping. If you want to stop seeing me then I'm cool with that. Hell I can't be caught with you in public, you know the rules."

Ebony started to cry, she was faking. She knew that Tommy didn't like to see her cry but tonight for some reason Tommy wasn't paying her any mind. He left Ebony standing there in the house looking stupid. Ebony ran after him and got in the car. Tommy drove fast doing 90 mph to Ebony's house. He gave her $500 dollars and told her to get out of his car and that he will call her when he feels like it. Ebony was pissed off because she went from being his side chick to his whenever I feel like it chick. She went in the house and called her cousin Rio and was more than ready to take all his cash and run off.

Two hours later Tommy was home, he came in, and tried to give me a kiss but I stopped him. I didn't feel like being phony. He didn't trip instead he went to take a shower. I sat at the dinner table and waited for him to join me. We both ate in silence. "Tia, we can't be sitting here all quiet and shit," said Tommy.

That was my cue. "Tommy if you're not happy with me, why be bothered. After all that we've been through I'm never enough for you. I fucked with you when you were locked up and everyone said fuck you. What do I get in return? A funky ass ring that really doesn't mean shit but looks really nice on my hand. I cook, clean, give you sex, and make my own money. I'm not doing anything wrong, there isn't anything wrong with me. As long as you keep dealing with her you can forget about sleeping with me. You out here just sleeping with random bitches that you don't even know. You don't know if they have anything or not all you care about is a big ass. I'm done talking about it and you're free to leave if you don't want to be here. I'm so fucking serious Tommy! At this point in my life I've had enough of the foolishness and for once I'm cutting all things off and people that doesn't make me happy. If you're one of those people I don't give two fucks about cutting you off too!"

Tommy sat across from me and got up out his seat. He walked over to me and grabbed my hand apologizing about his behavior. He promised that he was going to change his ways and get back on track. Apart of me didn't believe him but I was ready to get my happiness back even if I did have to deal with Tommy's bullshit.

Chapter Fourteen

Kayla

Once those guards unlocked those gates I felt like a new woman. You know what they say, YOLO, You Only Live Once, and shit I felt like I had died and was brought back to life. I walked outside anxiously to see Smooth waiting for me. I made sure before I left that I looked nice. My hair was wavy from the braids that I took down in my hair. My light skin had a natural glow. My shape had snapped back after the baby and added a few pounds in all the right places. I skipped out of MCC and looked for Smooth's car. I heard a horn blow and I looked to see that it was Aaliyah waiting on me. I went to the car and got in.

"Hey bitch, my girl is out now!" Aaliyah said smiling.

"Hey girl, yes I am finally free. Where the hell is Smooth?" I asked getting straight to the point.

"He had some business to take care of and asked if I could pick you up instead," she said.

"I knew his stupid ass wasn't coming to pick me up. Fuck him and take me to my baby." I said with an attitude.

Aaliyah did just that. On the ride home she told me everything that was happening on the street. She tried to cheer me up but to be honest I wasn't surprised that Smooth wasn't there for me. Aaliyah drove out South and parked in front of a two flat brick building.

"Where are we?" I asked.

"This is where you live Kayla." Aaliyah said getting out of the car.

"The Southside?! I told Smooth specifically that I didn't want to stay out South. I'm a Westside girl." I said.

"Girl, shut the hell up and stop complaining. You're lucky that he even put you in one of his places and looked out for you. A lot of people will tell you all that they will do for you while you're locked up and once you're released you wouldn't be able to find them."

Aaliyah walked in the gate first and I followed behind her up the stairs. She rang the doorbell and Mrs. Jackson opened the door. I was surprised to see her maybe her son was inside as well.

"Hello Kayla welcome home." Mrs. Jackson said.

"Hello Mrs. Jackson," I said looking around for my baby.

The carpet was white so Aaliyah and I removed our shoes. I could smell soul food cooking in the house. Mrs. Jackson walked in the back. I took a moment to look around the place and it was really comfortable.

"I hope that you like it. I got the colors that you asked me to get." Aaliyah said.

I was just about to tell her how much that I loved the place but I was caught off guard by the sight of Variyah. Mrs. Jackson handed her to me. "Thank you so much for taking care of my baby girl." I said.

"You don't have to thank me." She said.

I sat down on the white sectional with Variyah in my arms. She was so juicy and very pretty with her brown skin and thick brows just like her father. I kissed her small hands and feet, hell I smothered her with kisses. Variyah smelled so fresh just like Baby Magic. Aaliyah left us both alone in the living room and went in the kitchen with Mrs. Jackson. I talked to Variyah as if she understood what I was saying.

"Hey beautiful mommy misses you so much. You look so cute just like a little doll. I want to apologize to you for being absent in your life for the first three months. I hope that you can forgive me. I will never leave you again. I promise to always be here from this point on. It's me and you against the world, Variyah. I will always protect you so that you don't have to grow up like I did. I will provide for you so that you don't have to do the things that I had to do. I love you, I love you, I love you!" I cried as I smothered her with kisses.

Variyah spoke back to me in her baby language. I spoke back pretending to act like I knew what she was saying. She was swinging her arms and talking.

"She loves to talk," said Mrs. Jackson.

I didn't realize that she was watching us.

"I don't know where she gets that from all she does is talk. She's not much of a crybaby so you don't have that problem."

"I love to talk, sometimes I could talk too much." I said smiling.

Mrs. Jackson laughed. "The food is ready and you could eat whenever you like." She said.

I didn't waste any time going to the kitchen to eat. The smell of the food was calling my stomach. Mrs. Jackson made baked and fried chicken, ham, greens, cornbread, dressing, yams, macaroni and cheese, plus a strawberry cheesecake. I thanked her for cooking all of this for me. This was the first time in a long time that I was quiet. Aaliyah and Mrs. Jackson talked and Variyah sat in her bouncer talking as well. I was thinking about where Smooth could be. I know his ass better show up soon.

Meanwhile

"Ciara, Smooth is here. He's waiting for you in the front. Do you want me to tell him to come back here?" London asked.

"Yes, can you please ask him to come in my office?" I said.

London went back out and I could hear her tell Smooth that it was fine to go to my office. It was a busy Friday at Bella's Boutique. Tonight Kevin Hart was going to be live at the United Center and women flocked in here left and right trying to find something to wear tonight. Smooth walked into my office smiling surprising me with flowers and lunch. I felt like the luckiest woman in the world right now.

"Hey Blackbone, I thought that I'd surprise you with lunch since you don't have time to step out." He said.

I got up to give him a kiss and hug. "Thank you so much husband. The flowers are very beautiful." I smelled them and placed them inside the vase. I poured my drinking water into the vase. "I see that you brought my favorite, Chick Fil A."

"Do you mind if I have lunch with you?" Smooth asked.

"No I don't mind at all have a seat. Are you ready for tonight?" I asked.

"Yes I am, maybe I should be asking you that question."

"I stay ready so that I don't have to get ready. I can't wait to see him. I know he's going to give us a good show." I excitedly said.

"Yeah that's my man, he's a funny dude. Damn slow down you eating too fast like you starving." He said.

"I am I haven't eaten anything today, me or London. Did you bring London something to eat too?" I asked Smooth.

"Yes, I did you know that I'm not that type of guy. London is out front eating and helping the customers." Smooth's cell phone vibrated and he answered, "Hello, okay, I'm up at Ciara's boutique having lunch with her." I looked at him trying to figure out who he was talking too. Smooth looked up and said, "My mother said Hello."

I smiled, "Tell her I said Hey." Smooth talked for another minute and ended his call.

"Look at you making a mess. You have mayonnaise all on your cheek. Let me get that for you." Smooth got up and licked the mayonnaise off my cheek and gave me a kiss. We kissed as he placed me on top of my desk pulling up my dress.

"Lock the door." I said.

He locked the door and dropped his pants. Smooth entered me, this was the first time that we had sex in my office. He sucked on my breast as I dug my nails into his back. I moaned softly because I didn't want anyone to hear us. Smooth grabbed my hips and fucked me harder. I knew that he was about to nut. Two minutes later we both came at the same time. I gave him a kiss and thanked him for the lunch and the dick. Smooth left and I straightened myself up before I stepped back out front.

"Do you have this dress in a medium?" Cherish asked London pointing to the dress that was on the mannequin.

"Yes we do as a matter of fact that is our last medium." London reached for the stick so that she could take down the mannequin.

Smooth walked out zipping up his pants getting Cherish attention.

"Let me help you out London," said Smooth. He took the mannequin down for her.

"Thank you Smooth and thanks for the lunch." London said.

Smooth, damn that name sounds familiar. Cherish looked at him and suddenly it kicked in that this was Kayla's baby daddy. London handed her the dress and asked if she needed to try it on, Cherish told her no. Cherish stood in line waiting her turn to pay for her clothes. Kayla did mentioned that his wife owned a boutique. Ciara walked out to help London and took the next customer in line. When it was Cherish turn to pay a female walked into the boutique and said, "Hey Ciara," and that confirmed everything. Wow I can't believe that I'm actually seeing the both of them and shopping in her boutique. Cherish paid for her dress and left. Damn I can't wait to tell Kayla.

Back at Kayla's House

Mrs. Jackson finally left leaving me, Aaliyah and Kayla alone. I was so happy because for a minute I thought that she staying here to keep an eye on me. Aaliyah went out to buy me a new cellphone and the first person that I called was Smooth. He answered the phone because he didn't know the number.

"Hello what's up baby daddy?" I asked.

"What's up?" Smooth said sounding dry.

"Thank you, my new place looks nice. When are you coming over?'

"Where is Variyah?" Smooth sounded irritated and I didn't give a damn.

"Variyah is right here, she's cool. If you so concerned about her, then you would be here." I said.

"Kayla, why do you always have to talk shit? You not going to be happy till I hit you in your mouth! I will be by there to see Variyah when I get a chance." **Click.**

His hoe ass hung up the phone on me and I called him back once, but he didn't answer. Fuck Smooth I don't have time to be playing games with him.

"Girl is Smooth still acting stupid?" Aaliyah asked.

"Yes I'm so sick of his shit!"

"Girl fuck him and tell me how we about to make this money. I am on my last few dollars and I need to check some paper." Aaliyah said rubbing her fingers together.

"When I talk with my friend Cherish, I will have her break everything down to you. She can explain it better than I can."

"Call her now! She is the person that you should be calling. Smooth is going to do Smooth."

I called Cherish and she answered. She was happy to hear from me and told me that she had to tell me something. I stopped her in her brakes and told her that Aaliyah was interesting in making money too. Cherish didn't mind and said that she will be by tomorrow to explain everything in person and that she doesn't like to talk on the phone. I told Cherish that I will call her back once Aaliyah leaves so that we could talk in private. One hour later and two bottles of feeding Variyah, Aaliyah went home and Variyah was sleep. I thanked Aaliyah for doing a great job in decorating my place. After she left, I called Cherish back to find out what she wanted to tell me.

"Girl Chicago is too small, tell me why I was shopping at Bella's Boutique today and I didn't have no idea that it was Ciara's place. Your baby daddy Smooth was in there too." Cherish said.

"Really? Around what time was this?" I asked.

"It was in the afternoon, like around 1p.m. I was like damn wait till I tell Kayla. Girl your baby daddy is fine. Anyway I can't really talk to long because I'm about to go see Kevin Hart tonight, but how are you and Variyah?" Cherish asked.

"We're both fine. I'm not going to hold you up, I will see you tomorrow like we planned." I said.

"Yes see you tomorrow," said Cherish hanging up the phone.

After Cherish told me that she ran into Smooth up at his wife's boutique, I immediately called him. Once he again, he didn't answer and I bet that he was at home with his family. I envied that bitch Ciara because after doing a year bid for him I still didn't have his heart. I wondered what they were doing and if they were going to the comedy show as well. If I had a car, I would be on some stalking shit right now. The more that Smooth ignored me the more that I hated him. I wanted to be immature and send him an angry text message but that would be what he expects from me. Instead I watched television while my baby girl was sleeping. I was blessed to be out and I didn't need him to stress me out. Smooth knew where to find me and when he was ready to show up I will be here. It was 9 p.m. and Variyah woke up crying, I changed her diaper and fed her again. She thought it was play time but I put her back to sleep. After that, I soaked in the tub and laid back sipping on some wine. I thought about Smooth and played with my pussy. I craved for him and wanted him badly. I missed him so much and wish that I was his wife instead of her by 11 p.m. I was asleep.

Chapter Fifteen

Smooth

Kayla's crazy ass was out less than 24 hours and already driving me crazy. I have fifty-six missed phone calls from her crazy ass. During the comedy show I had my ringer turned off because I knew that she was going to be blowing my phone up. It was late the comedy show started at 7 p.m. but he didn't come out until 9 p.m. I made sure that Ciara was safely in the house before I pulled off. I told her that I was going to make some runs and will be back shortly. She told me to be safe and I showed her my two guns that I had on me and kissed my queen before I pulled off. It took me an hour to get from my house in Westchester to Kayla's place out South. I parked my whip and hopped out of the car. I didn't call her I popped up because I had the right to do that. I had the keys to the place so I let myself in. Once I got inside I took off my shoes and walked through the house to make sure that anyone but Kayla and Variyah was there. I checked in Variyah's room and she wasn't in her crib so that meant that she was in the bed with her mom. Kayla was knocked out sleep with Variyah on top of her chest. I sat down at the end of the bed and Kayla moved. It took her a while to realize that someone was sitting on her bed and she jumped up.

"Smooth, what are you doing here? What time is it? You scared me!" Kayla said rocking Variyah who was now awake, crying.

"I told you I was coming by when I had time. Its 12:27 a.m." I said taking Variyah away from her and rocking her back to sleep. Kayla gave me hug and rested her head on my shoulder and stared at Variyah.

"We're one big happy family." She said.

I pushed her off me. "Kayla don't start that shit! You know it's really about Variyah and that I'm not in love with you."

"Why not Smooth? Look at me!" Kayla jumped out of the bed and removed her pajamas exposing her naked body. She turned around so that I could see her ass. "You know that you miss all of this! You know that I look good."

I'm not going to lie she looked really good that she made my dick rise. I can see that she got a little thicker as well. I just can't go back down that lane with her. Once I put that dick back on her, she would go bananas. I took Variyah into her room and laid her down in her crib. When I went back into Kayla's room, she was laid across her bed with her legs wide open. I shook my head.

"Kayla, why you doing all that? You know I can't be fucking around with you like that." I said.

"Smooth, you know that I love you. I proved that by doing that bid. I haven't had any dick for a year. Please fuck me." Kayla begged.

"I can't give you this dick. You already crazy and once we start having sex again you would be insane. I can't risk getting caught up in your games." I said.

"Smooth, why do you treat me like this? I know why you do, it's because I allow you too! I'm so tired of arguing and fighting with you. Let's make love and not war."

Kayla got up from the bed and seduced me. I sat down and she pulled my pants down and started sucking my dick. It was so wrong but it felt so right. She did a great job, spitting and licking on it. Her head bobbed up and down like a bobble head.

"Shittt!" I said as I exploded. Kayla kept on sucking and swallowed me up. She went to go get me a wet towel, came back, and cleaned me up just like she used to do.

"I miss you so much and I promise not to act crazy. You just be pushing my buttons sometimes and that's when I start tripping out and shit."

"Kayla just because you just sucked my dick it doesn't mean shit. I don't want you to start with that crazy shit. And when you call my phone and I don't answer you don't have to keep on calling me. That only aggravates me more to the point that I don't want to talk to you at all."

"If you answer the first time that I call, then maybe I shouldn't have to keep on calling you. You ignore me and that hurts my feelings," said Kayla.

"Oh we working with feelings now?"

"I always have been. Unfortunately for me you haven't." Kayla said.

"But what I can't understand is how can you love someone who's not in love with you?"

I went in my pocket and counted my money giving Kayla $7000 dollars. "Here you go, get yourself something to ride in. It's plenty of more where that came from. As far as the rent and the bills you don't have to worry about that because this is my place. Kayla, I don't want you to think that I'm just giving you money and doing all this for you. I'm doing it for my baby girl and making sure that she's straight. You got that?"

"Yes, yes, yes. I understand." She said. Kayla took the money, counted it, and put it to the side.

"Let me get out here it's getting late." I stood up to go and my phone vibrated. It was Ciara so I answered. Kayla rolled her eyes I talked to her on the phone. Before I left, I kissed Variyah and headed for the door. Kayla watched me through the vertical blinds as I got into my car. Once I got inside, I pulled off and speed down the block. I didn't even noticed that someone was following me. The car followed me and was on my ass. Before I could get to my gun, he fired several shots. I managed to shot back unaware if it hit him or not. He fired back and was able to get close enough to me that I managed to hit him a few times. Suddenly, another car hit me and caused me to crash into a park car. I was able to get out of my car and crawl away. I was hit in my neck, chest, and leg. The shooter pulled up to my car, got out, and grabbed the duffel bag of money that was in the trunk of my car. He ran up on me and was prepared to fire, but a lady screamed, "Call 911! Call 911!"

He ran off, jumped into his car. I pulled out my cell phone to call Ant, "That nigga caught me slipping, I'm shot!" I said before I passed out.

Ciara

Flying down California Avenue frantically, I almost hit several cars as I flew through red lights. I didn't care if I received 100 red light tickets in the mail, I was going to see about my man. As I received a phone call from Ant that Smooth has been shot multiple times, my heart dropped. I feel as though it stopped beating. I approached 15th and made a quick left pulling up in front of the ER at Mount Sinai Hospital. I rushed inside leaving my car still running with the keys in the ignition.

"Excuse me nurse I'm looking for Eric Jackson!" I said frantically.

"Mrs. Please calm down, may I ask who you are?" The nurse replied back nonchalant.

"Bitch you keep calm and I'm his wife, Ciara Jackson! Point me in the right direction before I go off in here!" I yelled pointing my fingers in the nurse's face.

"Mrs. Jackson he's in surgery right now. Can you please have a seat in the waiting area?"

"Can you please tell me what's going on with my husband?" I cried.

"Mr. Jackson was brought here with multiple gun shot wounds. The doctors are performing surgery on him now. That's all the information that I can give you at this moment. Can you please calm down and have a seat in the waiting area and someone will be there to talk with you shortly."

I exploded, "Bitch why do you keep telling me to keep calm and have a seat?! Where is my husband?! I want to see him!"

Two lame ass security guards walked up and told me to have a seat before they put me out. "I wish that a muther fucker would put me out! Who is going to make me leave?!"

Kelly rushed inside, "Ciara is everything cool? What's going on? Please get back I can handle it from here!" Kelly said to the two guards. I fell in my best friend arms crying.

"Everything is going to be fine. Let's go and have as seat and wait for everyone to get here. Niecy is parking your car and she will be inside soon," said Kelly.

We took a seat a seat in the waiting area and everyone watched us like they were watching show. Denise joined the both of us and she gave me a hug.

"I don't know what happen, or what is going on." I cried.

I can tell by the look in Kelly's eyes that she was aware about what was going on. She was about to speak but an outburst at the nurse's station got our attention.

"God please don't let my man die. God please my baby girl needs her father!" Another female who was holding a baby cried at the nurse station. I looked and wiped the tears from my face because I couldn't believe my eyes or what I just heard.

"Is that Kayla and Aaliyah?" Kelly asked.

It was her and she was holding a baby that resembled Smooth. I took off so fast toward the nurse's station that it was too late for anyone to stop me. All I could hear was Kelly yelling. "Ciara Noooo! Oh my god! Please don't kill her!" Kelly yelled.

She was holding the baby but I didn't care I smacked that bitch so hard that she didn't see it coming. "What the fuck! Aaliyah hold my fucking baby!" Kayla said giving her baby to Aaliyah. I punched the hoe in her face three times, I was waiting for her to steal on me first. Kayla swung and hit me a few times. I slammed her down and started stomping her. I was just about to punch her in the face again but security had grabbed my little ass and held me back.

"Hoe you have some nerves coming up here talking about your baby needs her father! Bitch that isn't Smooth's baby!" I yelled at Kayla.

Kayla was still on the floor, she had blood all over her face from her busted nose. "Bitch this is his daughter! Meet Variyah Jackson!" Kayla said pointing at Aaliayh and her baby girl who was now crying.

"Bitch stop lying and go find your real baby daddy!" I yelled trying to get away from security to tag her ass one more time.

"She's not lying Ciara, that is Smooth child," said Aaliyah.

"Who is even talking to you Aaliyah?! Mind your business and worry about yours!" Kelly said.

"Kelly shut up before I beat your ass up in here!" Aaliyah said.

"Aaliyah shut me! You shit starting bitch, always in the middle of some bullshit! That's why Vell fucking the girl that lives next door to you!" I yelled and started laughing.

Aaliyah handed Kayla back her baby and tried to come for me but Niecy blocked us. "Yes bitch I bet that you didn't know that!" I yelled.

"If you don't believe me ask Mrs. Jackson." Kayla said pointing at Mrs. Jackson who had just walked in and was standing there looking. I looked over at Mrs. Jackson and she had a look of sorrow on her face.

"Ciara I can explain." Mrs. Jackson said.

"You know what fuck all of you and you can't explain shit to me!" I yelled.

Security escorted me, Kelly, and Niecy to another area of the hospital. I could hear Kayla in the background as we walked away.

"Surprise Bitch!" Kayla yelled.

Two hours later the doctor came out. Everyone stood up, except me and Kelly. I was crying and Kelly was holding me.

"Can I please speak with the wife of Eric Jackson in private please?" The doctor asked.

"Yes." I cried as we walked down the hall.

"Hello Mrs. Jackson I'm Dr.Kumar the one that operating on your husband Eric Jackson. He was shot three times, once in the neck, in the arm, and in the leg."

"Oh my god!" I cried.

"I have good news, the surgery was successful your husband is doing fine. We were able to remove the bullets.

He's now resting and being sedated in the Recovery Room."

"Can I see him?" I asked.

"I'm afraid that you can't for another 24 hours sorry. I suggest that you go home and get some rest."

"Thank you so much Dr. Kumar." I said.

"You're welcome." He said and walked away back behind the double doors.

I walked back to the waiting area and everyone was waiting to hear what the doctor had to say.

"Ciara is everything fine?" Smooth's mother asked.

I didn't really want to answer her because I was upset with her. I turned to everyone else, "Yes he's fine, the surgery was successful. We can't see him until 24 hours." I said.

Everyone was happy and prepared to leave to go home. Before leaving the hospital, I put a restriction on Smooth's visitors. I went home and Kelly stayed with me and didn't want to leave me alone. My mother had my children and I called to check on to see how they were doing.

"Hello mom I just made it back home." I said.

"Is everything fine Ciara? How is Eric doing?" Brenda asked.

"Yes he's fine but I can't see him till tomorrow. Do you mind keeping the children again?" I asked.

"Thank you god! I was really praying for him. I don't mind keeping them."

"Thank you so much mom and if you need a break just let me know. Kelly or Niecy doesn't mind coming to get them." I said.

"Oh no were just fine. You just make sure that you get some rest. I love you and I will keep praying for you both."

"I love you too mom, good night."

Kelly was on the phone talking to Ant. I went in the kitchen and boiled me some water in the tea kettle for a cup of tea. After that I stood at the kitchen counter and just remained quiet. I didn't hear Kelly come in the kitchen.

"Ciara are you okay?" Kelly asked.

"Kelly, I'm thankful that God has spared his life but deep down inside I'm so angry and hurt right now. To find out that my husband has another baby by another woman while he is fighting for his life is crazy. How can I be there for him right now? Smooth did it again and this time I'm not staying by his side. There is no explanation this time! I'm so damn sick and tired of all the bullshit. Once he comes home, I'm leaving him for good!" I said.

"Ciara, I totally understand and I don't blame you. Whatever you choose to do is your decision and I support you and have your back. I just can't believe that he has done it again and a woman can only take so much," said Kelly.

"Not only that but you hid it again and this time your mother knew. I just want to know how long they were going to play this game." The tea kettle whistled and Kelly made us two cups of tea. We went to sit down on the couch and continued to talk and drink our tea.

"So that means that Kayla was pregnant while she was incarcerated. That's how he was able to keep it away from you. You know how I keep my ears to the streets. Kayla had to just get out and she doesn't really fuck with too many females and always been private. I knew that bitch Aaliyah was not to be trusted. I bet you all this time she knew all about it. I kept telling y'all that she rubbed me the wrong way." Kelly said.

"Now that I'm thinking that explains why the numerous of times I tried to go by Smooth's mother house that she will always be too busy to see me. She always had an excuse and Smooth would defend her. Plus it was another time when the children came home from spending the day with her and Erica mentioned that she held a baby." I cried.

"Ciara don't cry. I know that it hurts right now but you can't allow them to get to you."

"That's some dirty and foul shit Kelly. How could he do this to me all over again?!"

"Ciara only Smooth know that answer. You can either let this situation break you down and rip you apart. Or you can move on with your life and start all over. Right now what's important is that Smooth is alive and that you don't have to bury him. Despite everything that has happened you or his mother, or his children didn't lose him. We are going to deal with one issue at a time." Kelly said.

Kelly was right because it could've been a lot worse and I'm so thankful that it wasn't. That still doesn't mean that Smooth isn't responsible for his behavior. I have to choose me this time and I choose to be happy. I no longer want to be a part of this triangle. I love Smooth but I love myself more.

Aaliyah

Ding Donk! Ding Donk! Ding Donk! I ran the bitch Victoria's doorbell and waited for her to answer. After Kelly confirmed of what I was thinking all this time was true I had to pay this whore a visit. I wanted to last night but I stayed over at Kayla's place by her side and Victoria finally came to the door.

"Bitch why are you on my front porch?!" Victoria asked standing in the doorway wearing a cami short set.

"I'm here to beat your ass!" **Punch!** I hit that bitch in her face and grabbed her by her long weave. I continued to hit her and we fought on her front porch. "Your whore ass was fucking my man all this time!" I said as I beat her ass. I was getting the best of her and she bit me. "Ouch! Oh you want to bite bitch?!" I hit Victoria in her mouth and jaw. I heard Vell's voice and he grabbed me and pulled us apart.

"Aaliyah what are you doing here?" Vell asked.

"Vell how could you?! Is this the dirty bitch that gave you herpes and then you gave it to me?!" I yelled.

"Let's go home babe. I'm sorry let me please explain everything," said Vell as he ushered me down her stairs.

Victoria ran inside her home and came back out with Vell's clothes and things and threw them on her lawn. "Since you leaving with that bitch, don't forget the rest of your things!"

Vell and I went inside my home and I smacked the shit out of him. **Smack!**

"I deserve that Aaliyah but I'm sorry. Please stop acting crazy and hear me out." He said.

"Hear you out?! Vell the girl next door, you couldn't fuck a bitch on the other side of town?! You know what's so funny I knew it all along. Vell why?! Why! Why! Why!" I screamed in his face.

"Because you're always nagging and I got tired of the arguing and fighting. I went somewhere that I can find peace. No matter how much I did for you it was never enough!" Vell said.

"Vell that's bullshit and you know it. Just as much as you did for me I did twice as much! So what if we argue, what couple doesn't! There is no excuse for you to go out and sleep with another woman period! Look at what happened when you did. You destroyed our family, gave me an incurable disease, and betrayed me. I've never cheated on you Vell, Never!"

"I'm so sorry Aaliyah, can we please work this out? I miss you and my daughter's so much. I promise to never hurt you again. Can you find it in your heart to forgive me? Please!" Vell said crying as well.

I cried and fell into his arms. I had flashbacks of all the good moments that Vell and I shared. Despite everything that Vell had done, I wanted to forgive him and start all over again. I just wanted my family to get back together as one. I was sick and tired of it all. It was time for a major change in my life.

"I want us to be a family again. The twins miss you so much and so do I. You need to get your act together and grow up for you and all of us. I nag and bitch all the time because what you do out on the streets affect us all." I said.

"You're right and I'm so stupid. I didn't realize that until now. I'm sorry that I have you out here fighting over me and it will never happen again." Vell said.

I decided to take him back and I really don't care what anyone has to say about it. I'm not strong enough to do it alone and raise the twins by myself. Day by day it was a struggle to stay strong, but I had to keep it together for my daughter's. Honestly, I don't know how single mothers do it every day because these two months were the hardest for me. I allowed Vell back in my life but as far as my heart, that was going to take a moment. Vell went to go and get his things from off of Victoria's lawn. She stood in her door way and looked as he picked up his items and returned back to my house. "Fuck you Vell! I was just using you for your money anyway!" She yelled.

Vell walked off and ignored her. I shook my head, "See I told you that bitch wasn't shit!" and I closed my door.

Vell showered and dressed. He had to leave to see about Smooth. I told him to be safe out there and don't do anything stupid because the twins need you to be around forever. After Vell left I gathered my thoughts and prayed to God.

"Dear God I know that we haven't talked in very long time but I know that you see everything that's going on. I've been such a bad person in my life and I know that I have did some hurtful things to others. I don't like the person that I've become. Please help me fix myself and get my life together. I no longer want to be this evil person that creates drama and confusion. Please remove all those in my life that don't mean me any good. Please help me control my anger. Please help me become a better mother and provider for my daughter's. Please teach me to forgive. Please protect the father of my children. Last but not least, please forgive me off all my sins. I'm ready to allow you into my life, I need you. Amen."

Chapter Sixteen

Ciara

"What do you mean I'm not allowed to see him?! That's the father of my child!" An angry Kayla yelled at the nurse's station.

"Sorry Miss but you're not allowed to see him. His visitor's are restricted." The nurse said.

"Is there anything that you do? Please I really have to see him." Kayla pleading and begged.

"No Miss there isn't anything that I could do, sorry," said the nurse.

I walked up, "Hello, I'm Ciara Jackson. I'm here to see my husband Eric Jackson." I handed the nurse my identification. She looked at it and buzzed the doors.

"Thank you Mrs. Jackson your free to go inside," said the nurse.

"You hear that the WIFE!" I said to Kayla.

Security walked up and stood in middle of the both of us.

I walked thru the doors and went to see my husband. I didn't have time for Kayla right now. Priorities first and that she will never be.

Kayla was standing there looking stupid, "It's cool Ciara, he won't be there for long. You just need to accept the fact that Smooth is both our man!" Kayla said pissed off because she couldn't see Smooth.

"No bitch you're just a Bum with a baby!" I said and walked off.

I walked inside Smooth's room to find his mother Mrs. Jackson sitting in the chair next to his bedside. Smooth was sleeping and snoring.

"Good morning Ciara." Mrs. Jackson said.

"Morning." I said back dryly.

"Ciara, do you mind if I speak with you in private out in the hall?" She asked.

"I don't mind."

We both stepped out of the room and in the hall. I waited to hear what Mrs. Jackson had to say.

"Ciara, I want to say I know that it looks like I'm in the middle of this and I would like to explain. Yes I was aware Eric's child and I took care of her. No I wasn't happy that he had another child with another woman that's not his wife but what's done is done and we can't do anything about that. When my son came to me for help, I couldn't deny him or my granddaughter. I didn't accept or support the situation, I was only looking out for the baby. The child doesn't have anything do with all of this foolishness. I demanded that Eric tell you several times but he never did. I wanted to tell you so many times but it wasn't my place to do so." Mrs. Jackson said.

"Mrs. Jackson, I'm not going to lie at first I was angry and upset with you. But after thinking about if I was in your shoes, I would've did the same thing for my son. I can't fault you because Eric is a grown man and is in control of his actions." I said.

"I deeply apologize for my son's actions. I really hope that you two can work all of this out and don't let it kill your marriage."

I laughed. "Right now, I'm here for my husband because he needs me. I will deal with that matter when the time is appropriate." I said.

I walked away and went back to have a seat inside the room. I know that everyone is wondering what Ciara is going to do. Is she going to stay? Is she going to leave? Honestly, I felt like my life was a big soap opera. Mrs. Jackson left to go home and told me to have Smooth call her as soon as he wakes up. I stood by Smooth's bedside and cleaned his face with a wet washcloth. He was sweating a lot, but the air was very comfortable inside the room. Maybe it was all the medication that they were giving him. Hours had passed and I was sitting watching television when Smooth woke up.

"Hey baby," Smooth said still sounding groggy.

"Hey Smooth, how are you doing?" I asked him wiping his forehead off with the wash cloth.

"In pain and really thirsty. How long have you been here?" Smooth asked touching his neck where he had been shot.

"Don't touch anything. I've been up here since 8 a.m this morning and it's going on 12 p.m." I pressed the call light and his nurse came in.

We asked her for pain medication and ice chips because Smooth had to be medically cleared to drink or eat anything. Smooth set up in bed and I fluffed his pillows and propped them back under him. He was weak and helpless. The nurse came back in and gave him his medication and ice chips. Smooth dumped the cup of ice chips into his mouth. The phone in his room began to ring and he answered the phone. The volume was up loud and I could hear that it was Kayla on the other end of the phone. He hung up the phone but she called back several times.

"Who is that your girlfriend or should I say baby momma Kayla that keeps on calling you?" I asked him.

Smooth's eyes got wide with shock. He had a look of sorrow on his face. At this moment I really didn't care and wanted to smother his ass with one of them pillows.

"Ciara, I'm so sorry. I never meant for any of that to happen." Smooth said.

"Smooth save it right now this is not the time or place to discuss that situation. You're just going to make me even angrier and I just might fuck around and kill you!" I said.

His phone rang again but this time I answered it. "I'm only going to tell you this once! Fall back bitch and stop calling up here. He doesn't want to talk to you! How stupid can you be?! Why don't you see about your crying baby in the background?!"

"Ciara, fuck you and put my baby daddy on the phone." Kayla said.

"Girl, you sound silly as hell! Kayla please find you someone else to play with before I beat your ass again!"

Smooth was telling me to hang up the phone on her and to stop going back and forth. "You see what happens when you fuck with thots?!" He grabbed my hand with the little strength that he had but I snatched it away. I couldn't look him in his eyes because I just might slap him. "Oh I almost forgot to tell you to call your mother back." Smooth called his mother back and while he was on the phone with her Dr. Kumar walked in.

"How are you doing Eric?" He asked him.

"I'm doing fine just in a little pain that's all," said Smooth.

"That's very understandable. I came to check on you early this morning when your mom was here but you were still sleeping. Right now I'm going to check on the wounds to make sure that they look normal. Ciara, I must warn you that this is going to be graphic but you can stay in the room if you like," said Dr. Kumar.

"I'm fine I think I can handle it." I said.

Dr. Kumar removed the bandage from his neck and I damn near wanted to pass out. Smooth had a golf ball sized hole on the side of his neck. The bandage was soaked with blood and he needed a fresh one. Whoever shot my husband, they were certainly trying to kill him.

"Everything looks good." Dr. Kumar said. He cleaned the wound with gauze and applied a new bandage. He examined him making sure that everything was fine. After Dr. Kumar left, Ant, Red, and Vell came to visit him. I left the room to give them their privacy. I didn't want to be in the room while they were discussing business. I made a phone call to our insurance company to file a claim for Smooth's car. That was done and after that I had to call around to find out where exactly was his car. I found out that the police still had it and needed it another day to investigate. I called my mother to check on her and the children and told her that Kelly will be there to pick them up. Now that I had that covered I called London to see how everything was going up at my boutique and she was fine. I thanked her for all of her help and told her that I will return next week and she will have a week off as well. You know London declined but I was going to make her and treat her to a nice getaway for her and her man. I don't know how much longer Smooth will be in the hospital or if he had to do rehabilitation. Before I stepped back inside the room, Kanye called me and I smiled. I went outside to take his call. When I heard his voice, it felt as though all my pain went away. Kanye asked how I was doing and I told him everything that had happened but I didn't mentioned the baby by his side chick. He felt sorry that I had to go through all of this and gave his condolences.

Kayla

Ciara isn't shit but a hater. It's cool I kind of figured that she was going to pull that stunt on me to keep me from seeing Smooth. Like I told her Smooth isn't going to be in the hospital forever and when he does get out I will still be around. I wanted to flatten Ciara's tires but there were too many cameras and people going to and from the hospitals. I called Cherish to come right back to the hospital to scoop me. She had dropped me off and kept Variyah as well. I called Aaliyah earlier this morning but she didn't answer. I don't know what was going on with her. Once Cherish picked me up we went back to my place to discuss business. I called Aaliyah again and this time she answered.

"What's up Aaliyah? I've been calling you all morning. My friend Cherish is over here. Remember I was telling you about the lick? Are you ready to make this money girl?" I asked her sounding excited.

"Kayla, I'm going to have to pass. I got back with Vell and working on getting my family back together," said Aaliyah.

"That's cool but please don't tell me that you let Vell get inside your head. You can still make this money and spend time with your family."

"It's not about Vell getting in my head or about the money. I'm just working on being a better and positive person." Aaliyah said.

"So what exactly are you saying Aaliyah? Because if you don't want to be my friend anymore that's your decision. Just say it and stop being fake!" I said.

"Kayla, I can't be associated with you anymore. The path I'm trying to take I can't allow any negative energy around me. I still love you like a sister Kayla."

"Aaliyah whatever you choose to do is fine with me. You will always be my sister. I wish you nothing but the best. Call me if you need me, goodbye," I said.

I wanted to cry but right now wasn't the time. I told Cherish that my friend wasn't going to be down and that meant more money for me. Cherish taught me everything and by the end of the day I was ready. The only problem I had was that I didn't have a car. I wanted to buy one with the cash that Smooth had gave me but that wasn't much. There wasn't any telling when Smooth was going to be released from the hospital. I called up there several times and tried to talk to him but Ciara was still up there. I fucking hate that bitch. I just want her to go away. If I had a car, I would ride up there and beat her monkey ass. Then Aaliyah talking about some life changing bullshit. The only one I had left in my corner was Cherish. I hope this card cracking shit pays off and is beneficial. But my man being shot up and in the hospital, I needed to check all the bread that I could make. It was late and I called Smooth again but he didn't answer. Damn! I felt like throwing my phone at the wall.

The next day I got up bright and early. I cleaned and dressed Variyah and called Cherish.

"Cherish, I need to get me a car today. Do you mind running me around to look for one?" I asked.

"No I don't mind. My man Lorenzo's friend owns a car lot on Western. I can run you up there. Are you ready now?"

"I'm ready to go."

"Cool. I will be there by 9 a.m. to pick you up."

Cherish was outside blowing her horn at 9:02 a.m. I grabbed Variyah, who was sitting in her car seat, and went out the door. We made it to the car lot by 10 a.m. and by 1p.m. I was pulling off the lot in a 2010 Jeep. It wasn't a 2015 or anything foreign but at least I didn't have to call anyone else for a ride. I thanked Cherish for taking me and once I hit the streets I had a visit to make. I pulled up in front of Aaliyah's house and called her.

"Hello Aaliyah, I'm sitting out in front of your house. Do you mind stepping out?"

Aaliyah peeped out of her curtains and stepped outside. She walked up to my jeep with a frown on her face.

"Do you like my new truck? I got it this morning." I said.

"What's up Kayla? Why did you pop up over my house?" Aaliyah asked with an attitude.

"I came by to see you and talk. Damn what's the big deal? What you too good to talk to me now?" I asked her.

"Look Kayla, you are involved in way too much bullshit for me. I just don't want to be down with any of it.

I'm getting older and really don't have time to be out here fighting and keeping up shit!" Aaliyah said.

"Just the other day you were that person on the exact same bullshit. What happened to fuck niggas get money? Why the sudden change? Please don't tell me that's it is Vell. Now that he's back in the picture you think that you're straight."

"It's not about Vell nor the money, you're missing the point. It's about me wanting a better future. Kayla the way you living, you'll be in and out of jail the rest of your life. What about your daughter? You need to slow down and change for at least the sake of her."

I noticed that a white 745 BMW pulled up and parked. It was the girl Niecy. Aaliyah walked over to her car and told her to give her minute. She walked back over to my truck.

"Kayla, I will see you around. I hope that you still don't mind me being Variyah's god mother," said Aaliyah.

"Oh I see what this is, that's your best friend now! You know what Aaliyah do you and you are no longer Variyah's god mother!"

I drove off upset and starting crying. You see that's the very reason why I don't fuck with many females today. I can't believe that she was still friends with that girl Niecy. The same person who is friends with another bitch that doesn't like you. But you talking about that you've changed. Girl, save that shit! Aaliyah bet not call me either when Kelly tag that ass because I'm not helping her. I went to the stores and started shopping and cracking my cards. By the end of the day I reported my earnings and made

$700 dollars off my first run. Not bad for my first day. I think I was going to love this job.

Chapter Seventeen

Ebony

My daughter was at my mother's house. Kimora was spending a lot of time with her grandmother. My mother enjoyed her when she visited. I guess she was making up for the times that she had missed out on me. I asked my mother to keep her for a week because I had to make this money. After Rio and I hit this lick, we were both leaving and going our separate ways.

My cousin Rio and I were chilling on my couch. The night that he had shot Smooth and took the duffle bag of money he dumped the car and drove straight to Texas. Rio was grazed by a bullet thankfully and not shot. It was close to $150,000 dollars inside the bag. Rio still wanted to set up Tommy, but I felt as though we had enough. The problem was Tommy wasn't fucking with me anymore. Yesterday I followed him and asked him not to cut me off. We were on the side of the road arguing. Tommy ran that script on me saying that he was working it out with his girl. As we were arguing a few cars slowed down to see what was going on. Tommy didn't like all the attention that he was getting so he jumped in his car and drove off. Rio was becoming anxious and was ready. I started setting everything up and told him the plan.

"Okay Tommy stops by his trap house between the hours of 7p.m. and 9p.m. We can park in the back and I will sneak in through the window that I left unlocked. We can wait for him to come in and have him open up the safe, kill him, and leave back out the back." I said.

"Cool so I will park in the back. Is the trap house in a busy area?" asked Rio.

"The neighborhood is quiet and don't too many people be outside. This will be very easy. In and out and were gone." I said.

Tommy was riding down the street and arguing on the phone with Tia. Tia's friend took a picture of Tommy and Ebony while they were arguing on the side of the road.

"Tia, I'm telling you that I stopped fucking with the bitch! You cool and don't have shit to worry about!"

"Tommy, I got your ass this time, not only that but I know the bitch you're messing with is a girl named Renee. She was a student at my one of my strip pole lessons and when I catch up with the bitch I'm fucking her up!" Tia yelled.

"Tia, I didn't know that she knew you. I'm sorry but I'm done dealing with her and I'm not going back and forth with you. Tia, I have to go and run in the spot real quick. I will talk to you when I get home."

Tommy hung up the phone on Tia while she was still talking. Tia was angry and hurt. She felt betrayed by Renee and all she seen was red. Tia called Ciara to tell her what was going on. She was the only one that was aware of what her and Tommy was going through. Ciara answered the phone on the first ring.

"Ciara, I'm sorry to call you about this. I know that you have a lot going on with Smooth."

"It's okay Tia tell me what's going on. I could talk Kelly and I are sitting in my house chilling and talking anyway."

"Let me make this quick. Look today the same friend that sent me a picture of Tommy last time sent me a picture again. This time she caught the girl's face and I'm about to send the picture to you."

"Okay let's see what this bitch look like," said Ciara.

I sent the picture to Ciara's phone.

"Let me know when you receive it. But check this out the whore that's messing around with Tommy is this female named Renee. She came for strip pole lessons at my dance studio months ago."

Ciara got the picture and looked at it. Her mouth dropped and she told Kelly to have a look at the picture as well. Tia could hear the both of them talking in the background.

"What's wrong? What are you and Kelly talking about? What's going on Ciara?"

"Tia, that's this girl named Ebony that set up Ant last year and fled away from Chicago," said Ciara.

"No her name is Renee."

Kelly snatched the phone out of Ciara's hand.

"Look Tia, that is Ebony. Her name isn't Renee. She's shiesty and 9 times out of 10 she's on some bullshit. She's the one who set up Ant and is now on the run. Please

tell me that you have an address on her or something!"
Kelly said.

"Oh my god! I have to call Tommy back and tell
him. I will call y'all back!" **Click!**

Tia called Tommy back while he was walking
inside the house. Tommy answered his phone.

"Tommy that bitch that you're fucking with is
Ebony from Chicago that had set up Ant. Her real name
isn't Renee it is Ebony!" Tia said.

"What, wait I'm lost. You telling me that her name
isn't Renee?" Tommy asked Tia but it was too late.

Tommy felt the gun in the back of his head and
dropped the phone. Ebony snatched the duffle bag out of
his hand.

"Surprise to see me?! Ha! Ha! Ha! Run all that cash
out of that safe!" Ebony said.

"You dirty bitch!" Tommy said.

"It's Ebony not bitch! Oh I forgot you thought it
was Renee." Ebony said laughing.

Tia heard everything and jumped in her car crying
and driving frantically to Tommy's trap house. She still
was trying to listen to hear what was going on but she
couldn't hear anymore. "Damn!" she cursed.

Tommy was at the safe acting like he couldn't
remember the combination but was really stalling for time.
He knew that Tia heard everything and had his back. They
have both talked and prepared for a moment like this,

"Nigga stop playing with me before I blow your head off and open up this muther fucking safe!" Rio said.

"I'm trying! I'm trying! I don't know why it's not working!" Tommy said.

"Tommy, I've seen you open up that safe plenty of times! Be a good boy and cooperate." Ebony said.

Tia had ten more minutes before she made it to the trap house. Ciara kept calling her phone but she couldn't answer. She pulled up to the house, jumped out of the car, and kick the door in. Tommy was slumped over, Tia began to cry harder. "Tommy!" she said. "Yes, Ebony ran out the back." Tia heard footsteps running in the back. She fired her gun. **Pop! Pop!**

Ebony shot back but missed Tia. **Pop! Pop!** Tia kept firing as she chased them out the back door and in the back yard. "Shit! What the fuck!" Ebony grabbed her leg and fell to the ground. Rio fired back and made it to the car leaving Ebony behind. Tia caught up with Ebony and pointed her gun to her head.

"Bitch, I don't know who the fuck you are but shit ain't sweet down here in Texas. You made have got away with that bullshit back in Chicago but it's over for you now!" Tia said.

"Bitch fuck you! That's why I killed Tommy and my cousin Rio shot up Smooth and took his shit too." Ebony said laughing.

Tia pulled the trigger. **Pop! Pop!** Two to the forehead.

Ebony's eyes rolled to the back of her head. Her head fell to the side and she was dead. Tia ran back inside the house to check on Tommy. Thankfully he still had a pulse. She got him out of the house and rushed him to the hospital.

Kelly

I heard the news that Ebony was finally dead. I wasn't surprised to hear that she was involved with Smooth shooting. Ebony was shiesty and willing do whatever she had to do for some money. With everything that was going on I decided that I wanted to get married right away. I didn't want to waste any more time. You never know when it's your time. You're here today and tomorrow you're gone. When Ant came home I will talk to him about it. I worry about Ant all the time when he's out in the streets. It has gotten to the point that he has to let me know every hour that he's okay. I almost lost him once and I can't go through that all over again. I'm already stressed out about my grandmother. Plus I have to be concerned about my brother as well. I sat in my room quietly in the dark just thinking. Sometimes that was the best thing to do. I will cry alone because I was afraid to let anyone see me weak, you know I'm known as being hard, tough, and strong. No matter how true that it is about me I've never been able to handle death well. I still mourn to this very day about Jasmine. I think about her all the time. It has been days that I will find myself often talking to her as if she was still her. I go to visit her and I will tell her about all the crazy things that are going on. Sometimes I wonder if things would be different if she was still alive. You know will I be so angry and always want to beat a bitch ass. I miss my best friend that became my sister so much. Ant came in and I could hear his footsteps coming up the stairs. He opened our bedroom door and seen me sitting in the dark crying.

"What's wrong Kelly? Why are you sitting in the dark? Did someone do anything to you?" Ant asked as he reached for his gun.

"No silly put that gun away. I was just thinking about a lot of things, that's all." I said.

"Thinking about what? Talk to me baby," said Ant.

"Anthony, I was thinking about that we should just get married right away. Skip the big wedding and reception. Let's do it like tomorrow."

"Whoa! Why do you feel this way? Why the sudden change?"

"Because of all the crazy things happening right now. My grandmother being sick. Smooth getting shot, Tommy down in Texas fighting for his life. I just don't want to lose you. Let's do it like tomorrow."

"Baby don't worry about that. Don't even think like that. I'm not going anywhere no time soon. I'm going to give you that big wedding. Your grandmother will be there. Smooth will be my best man. Tommy is going to make it. Let's think of the positive instead of the negative."

"How sure can you be of that, Ant? It's crazy out in the streets and you're out there every day. I will die if something happens to you. I almost lost you once and was ready to go to war for you. I love you so much and I worry about you Ant." I said crying.

"Kelly, I will die if something happens to you too but that's not going to happen. I love you shorty." Ant said and gave me a kiss. "You up in here in the dark tripping. No more weed or patron for you." Ant laughed and kissed me on my forehead.

"I still would like to push the wedding up." I said.

"Fine, if that would make you happy then let's do it. I can't have you around here sad and unhappy."

"Thank you Ant you're always spoiling me."

"You deserve it." Ant said.

Anthony and I made love and I did a good job of spoiling him back. Every night we made love like it was our time. You never know what could happen tomorrow. After we were done I watched Ant fall asleep first. Then I would bet down on knees and pray before I went to sleep.

The next day Ant and I met Marilyn and her boyfriend for lunch at Pappadeaux. Lately Ant has spending more time with his mom but he still wasn't too fond of Lorenzo. Ant said that he didn't trust him. He just went with the flow for his mother sake. We all were enjoying ourselves. For the first time we had a drama free date with the two. I just hope that it remains this way.

Meanwhile

Cherish and Kayla were shopping in Oak Brook Mall. They were busy cracking cards and buying everything that they could. They had been there since the morning and was ready to call it a day. They made it safely to Cherish car and loaded their things inside her trunk. They both jumped in.

"I'm hungry. Let's sit down and eat," said Cherish.

"Yes I'm starving! I have a taste for some Pappadeaux." Kayla said.

The two went to have lunch at Pappadeaux. When they got there it wasn't that crowded as usually because it was on a Wednesday afternoon. They were seated right away and followed their waiter. As they walked to their table Cherish seen Lorenzo sitting across the restaurant.

"I know that isn't Lorenzo sitting over there with another woman." Cherish said walking toward Lorenzo.

Kayla followed behind her. When they made it to the table Lorenzo had a shock look on his face.

"What's going on Lorenzo? Do you mind introducing me to your friends?!" Cherish said with her hands on her hips.

Kayla recognized Kelly and Ant right away but remained quiet. Lorenzo was looking stupid and caught up. He didn't even say anything.

"What's the matter? You can't talk now?! While since you can't talk let me introduce myself. I'm Cherish, Lorenzo's woman also the mother of Lorenzo's daughter, Laniyah." Cherish pointed, "You must be Marilyn, the older woman I heard that Lorenzo met while I was incarcerated."

"Yes I'm Marilyn and I wasn't aware that Lorenzo had a woman. I heard that you were in jail for a very long time and that he had custody of his daughter. I've been around your daughter several times. Lorenzo how could you do this to me?!"

"Lorenzo, you lied and told this woman that you're single and had her around my baby?!" Cherish picked up the butter knife from the table and tried to stabbed him. Lorenzo put his right arm in the air to block the knife and was stabbed in the arm.

Everyone turned to look at was going on and was in shock. Ant, Marilyn, and I got up from the table. I looked at Ant and the lock on his face wasn't good. I tried to grab his hand but it was too late. **Smack!** Ant smacked Lorenzo so hard that he knocked him out of his chair. I was waiting on his woman or Kayla to make a move but they didn't. We all left out of the restaurant, got in the truck, and pulled off. While driving out of the parking lot Oak Brook police pulled up and went inside. Marilyn was in the backseat crying quietly and I felt sorry for her.

Ant was pissed off that his mother was hurting. When we made it home, him and his mother talked alone. I left the both of them downstairs to have some privacy. I went upstairs in my room and called Ciara to tell her everything that had happened. I wouldn't have told her but the only reason why I did tell her was because Kayla was with the girl, Cherish.

Chapter Eighteen

Ciara

I finally met up with Kanye after I closed up the boutique for the night. He asked me to meet him at his home in Northbrook. When I made it there Kanye was waiting for me and looking so handsome. This was my first time at his home but certainly not the first time that he had invited me. His home was nice and big you can tell by the neighborhood that it wasn't cheap. I noticed quite a few boxes and I sat down on the couch and Kanye asked if I wanted something to drink but I declined. I just wanted to get straight to the point and share with him everything that has been going on. After telling him about my drinking problem, counseling, Smooth getting shot, and revealing that I found out that my husband had creating another love child, Kanye was in awe.

"Ciara, I see that you've been going through a lot. I must say that I wasn't prepared to hear all of this. I'm very sorry that you're going through all of this. How do you remain so strong?" Kanye asked.

"That's thing I appear to be strong but inside I'm breaking down." I just couldn't hold it in any longer and broke down and cried.

Kanye cradled me in his big arms. I just let everything out and cried so hard. I cried for about ten minutes before I could speak again.

"Ciara, you're too beautiful to be crying and too good of a woman to be going through all of this," said Kanye.

"I agree and that's why I'm filing for a divorce. I don't want to be married to him anymore. I have thought it over and I'm deciding to finally put me first. Tomorrow my husband will be released from the hospital. I'm going to tell him right away. I know that this will affect the children but I will be good." I said.

"Come and go away with me." Kanye said.

"What do you mean by go away with you?" I asked and was confused.

"Ciara, I've been trying to tell you this but my job promoted me and offered me a better position in Arizona. That's what I've been meaning to tell you. I will be leaving in one week."

"Congratulations Kanye that's great! Arizona, Wow! That explains all the boxes that I see now. I'm happy for you but sad that you're leaving."

"Ciara, you don't have to stay here, you can go with me. I'm in love with you and I can't leave you here in Chicago behind. I refuse too."

"Kanye even when I do leave Smooth I can't go away with you. I have children, a business that I have to run, and my mom and friends."

"You can start all over and Arizona is a great place to raise you children. Your mother and friends can come and visit. Ciara, I know that this is a lot to consider but can you at least think about it?"

"Kanye, I don't know this all a bit too much. I mean we haven't even made love yet. I care for you and I'm not going to lie I was falling in love with you. I think that you're asking for a lot from me right now."

"Alright Ciara, I don't want you to force you into doing anything that you don't want to do. As far as you and me never making love that's because you're still married and I will never disrespect your marriage. You will never do no such thing. You ask me to wait and give you time and I did. I'm sorry I was expecting to be promoted but I wasn't expecting my new position to be in Arizona. I really don't want this to end."

"Kanye, I will think about it. One week is right around the corner. Wow!"

"Ciara, I don't expect you to move in a week or right away. Of course I will have to get settled first. I know that moving to another state is a big decision. Please take your time to think about it. I'm not asking for much."

Kanye held me tight and we kissed. I'm not going to lie I wish that I could just run off with him and leave all my troubles behind but I can't. Married women can't do the same things as a single woman. Being with him right now I seemed more protected. Smooth never really gave me that 100% protection. When the other women and babies came along that went all out of the window. I was shocked to hear about all of this, I wasn't prepared. I see the saying is real life goes on and all this time I was asking Kanye to wait, he was leaving his life. I can't hold him back, I asked him to do that for too long already. I seriously had to make a change rather it be with Kanye or not. If I don't I will always keep putting myself in the position, to continually be in the same position. I chilled out with Kanye for another hour before I went home. I promised him that I was going to make his last week in Chicago the best before he left. The only thing we did was kiss but deep inside I know I wanted to do more. I had needs and lately I haven't been having sex because Smooth isn't able to. It was tempting and I was starting to go there so I decided that it was time for me to leave before we get to fucking on this couch. Kanye walked me to my car and opened the door like a gentleman. I sure was going to miss him.

The next day Smooth was released from the hospital. Ant, Vell, and Red picked him up from the hospital while I stayed home getting everything together. I was having a small gathering for Smooth, just family and close friends that I consider family. I had to be safe because the person that tried to kill Smooth was still out there and they haven't caught up with him yet. Smooth arrived home and was very happy to see everyone. He healed up pretty good but still had some weeks to go. His arm was in a sling and the leg that he had got shot in was in a cast so therefore he needed crutches. Erica and Eric Jr. ran up to their daddy giving him a big hug. They really missed their father so much. I never allowed them to see their father in the hospital while he was in that condition. It was already hard enough for me to tell them what was going on but with the help of my mother she told them in such a way that they understood. Smooth hugged them back and I helped him have a seat on the couch. Eric Jr. didn't want to leave his side so Smooth sat him on his good leg. Everyone was having a good time, eating, laughing, and socializing. I played along but deep down inside I was happy that Smooth was still alive. But I wasn't happy to be with him after all that has happened. Vell and Aaliyah were back together although I really don't rock with her I was still happy for them. I know you're wondering why I'm cool with her being inside my home, especially with her and Kayla being friends. Last week Aaliyah took it upon herself to apologize about her involvement in the Kayla and Smooth's situation. She went on to tell me that she isn't friends with Kayla any longer and that she's a changed person. What I did respect about Aaliyah was despite her and Kayla no longer being friends she didn't throw dirt on her name. That was proof that Aaliyah was changing. The old Aaliyah would have talked about Kayla, told all of her business, and sat back and watched me and Kayla battle. I still didn't really care to be her friend but I did accept her apology. Vell convinced and asked me to at least give her a try. Vell never asked me for anything so I did it for him. It showed that he was taking his relationship more serious. Vell said that Smooth was like a brother to him, and when you see him, you see Aaliyah. So I give it a try and that's the only reason why she is her. From the looks of things a lot has changed. Niecy, Kelly, and Aaliyah were having a conversation and they weren't arguing. Wow! I was shocked. I always knew that Kelly had it in her. Aaliyah better not get on her bad side ever again. Any way things were going fine it was getting late and unfortunately I was time for this small gathering to end. The fellas helped me clean up as much they could. I was tired and ready for everyone to go. I said good bye and thanked everyone that came. I thanked everyone for their love, prayers, and for being by my side when I needed them the most.

In The Cut

Kayla sat in her truck five houses down and watched the guest leave Ciara and Smooth's home. Angry that she hasn't seen or heard from Smooth ever since he has been in the hospital. I watched all the people leave Ciara's house. Apparently, she had Smooth a small welcome home party. Everyone got the news, but me, that he was out of the hospital. I called Mount Sinai earlier to find out that Smooth was released. I knew that it was coming soon beings that he was in the hospital for three in a half weeks. I called Smooth's mother and she was acting like she didn't want to tell me anything. For the last few weeks, I have been going through her in order to get anything from Smooth. Mrs. Jackson would come by to watch Variyah when I needed her to. She would also give me money for her and tell Smooth whatever I needed. I knew that she was going back reporting what was going on too, so I watched what I said and did around her. If Smooth thinks that this is the way that's it's going to be for 18 years, he has to be tripping. I became upset and took it upon myself to camp outside his home. I saw when they pulled up and everything. Smooth looked so helpless with the help of his friends. I felt so bad for my baby daddy that I almost cried and cared. I'm not going to lie, I had feelings for Smooth when I came home. I really thought that I had a chance to be with him. Lately, the way that he has been acting my feelings are slowing going away. I was so sure that Ciara was going to leave him and I will have him all to myself. Unfortunately for me, things didn't go that way. As a matter of fact, everything has changed. I couldn't believe that phony bitch Aaliyah was walking out of Ciara's house. "I should run that snake bitch over." I said to myself. I sat back and watched all the cute couples leave. Ciara, Smooth, and their children stood at the door waving good bye like a happy family.

Back at Ciara's Place

I was so happy that everyone had left. I cleaned up the place while Smooth bonded with our children in the living room. I really wasn't prepared for this moment of him coming home. It was now the time to address this daughter that he created with Kayla. I put the children to bed and Smooth took his time going up the stairs, one by one. The children were finally sleeping, peacefully. I walked in my bedroom and Smooth was struggling taking off his jeans. I went to help him.

"Smooth, I think its best that you wear sweat pants until your cast is removed. It would be a lot easier." I suggested.

"Thank you baby for helping me. You know that I love you." Smooth said.

I looked at Smooth like he was crazy. What's love got to do with it? He didn't love me while he was fucking Kayla. Enough was enough and I was ready to get everything off my chest.

"Smooth, I'm not with this fake shit." I said.

"What fake shit Ciara? What are you talking about?"

"Me pretending that I'm not hurt and hiding behind this mask. There isn't anyone around now I don't have to fake it now. After everything that we've been through,

Smooth, you go and do it again. What you thought that I wasn't going to find out? Then you drag your poor mother in your bullshit. Are there any more children out there that I should know about? Anything else that I need to know?" I asked him being serious.

"No there isn't any more children. Ciara, I know that I fucked up in the past but this was an accident." Smooth said.

"Smooth, you sound silly. What you accidently slid inside of her, without a condom, and got her pregnant?"

"No that's not what happened. I had on a condom but it busted. Look I'm sorry but if you want to talk about it, then I'm going to tell you the truth."

"You know what Smooth, I really don't care to hear your side. After all is said and done, that baby is yours. While you were in the hospital, I had the time to think about it all. You were back dealing with Kayla during the time that they raided her crib. I bet you thought that I didn't know about that. Ha! Ha! Ha! Just because you didn't tell me, didn't mean that I wasn't going to find out. She went to jail pregnant; therefore, she had no choice but to keep the baby. Because I know that if she wasn't in jail for a fact that you would've made her get an abortion."

"Ciara, I said that I'm sorry. Damn I fucked up and now you're pissing me off about this. I'm sorry. I fucked up." Smooth was agitated.

"Smooth, you do not get to raise your voice at me, nor have the right to be mad. You out here cheating on me and think that I'm suppose to just accept it. Bullshit! You know what's funny? It's not the cheating that's hurting me.

I'm hurt because you're actually romancing and having an emotional connection with your side chick. There's no difference than what you have with me. Hell, I'm in the same category but guess what? Smooth, I'm removing myself because I ain't fighting for a spot in nobody's life! I'm filing for a divorce. I'm tired of being unhappy and not being able to trust you. This is stressing me out and all too much for me!" I said removing my ring and putting it on the dresser.

"Ciara, you don't mean that, you're just upset right now and just talking. You're not going anywhere." Smooth said.

"Yes I am Eric! I'm tired and I'm fed up and there isn't anything that you could do or say about it!" I heard Eric Jr. crying. I went to go and check on him. He was crying for his daddy and asked if he could sleep with him. I took him into the room to sleep with his daddy. Smooth was talking but I didn't want to hear anything that he had to say. I left out our bedroom that we once shared and went to sleep in the guest room.

Monday morning I got up and prepared the children and myself for the day. I had to go to work earlier because I was receiving a new large shipment. I was dropping the children off to Mrs. Jackson. Smooth was sitting down watching television downstairs eating a bowl of cereal. The children and I told him goodbye. They kissed their daddy and Smooth tried to kiss me but I pushed his lips away.

"Are you going to be cool?" I asked him.

"Yes I will be just fine." He said.

I jumped in my car and dropped the children off to their grandmother's house and went to work.

I jumped up and out of the bed. I got Variyah dressed and ready. Today I was going to be on some bullshit. I wasn't going another day without seeing Smooth. I called Mrs. Jackson and lied and told her that I had a job interview and that I needed her to watch Variyah. She said that she didn't mind. I put on red sexy thong and bra set under my wrap dress and some red sling backs. I made it to her place around 11a.m. I walked Variyah to the door and I saw that Ciara's children were there as well. That was perfect. All I had to do now was swing by the boutique to see if wifey was at work. I pulled up at the boutique and I could see that Ciara was at work. Next I went to Smooth's house and I planned on surprising him.

Kayla

Smooth was starting to get tired. The couch was uncomfortable so he went back upstairs to get in bed instead. He took his time and hopped up the stairs. He was out of breath once he made it upstairs. Smooth turned on the 50 inch television and watched the movie 300. That was one of his favorite movies. He turned the television up loud and sat back and watched the movie.

I walked on Ciara's and Smooth's front porch. I played like I had a key, just in case the neighbors were watching and noticed me picking the locks. I walked inside and looked around the place. It looked very clean, like a family home. Ciara had nice taste. I was looking for

Smooth and I could hear the television from upstairs. I walked up the steps softly so that he couldn't hear me. I followed the sound of the television and peeped inside the room. Smooth was laying down watching a movie. He was wearing a Nike tee shirt and some gym shorts. I loosened up the string on my wrap dress and jumped inside the room.

"Surprise!" I said opening up my dress and exposing my body.

Smooth grabbed his gun and pointed it at me. "Kayla, how in the fuck did you get in here?!"

"Put that gun down silly. The front door was opened so I let myself in. Aren't you happy to see me?" I moved closer to Smooth.

Smooth lowered his gun. "Kayla, you're crazy as hell! You need to get out of my house! What the fuck is wrong with you?!"

"What do you mean what's wrong with me? I miss you and wanted to see you silly." I took Smooth's hand and rubbed it against my skin. "You know that you miss me." I looked over at Smooth's dick that was standing up. "See I told you that you miss me." I laughed and grabbed his dick.

"Kayla, you have to leave because if Ciara catches you in here she will kill you."

"Fuck Ciara! Besides she's at work anyway, I already checked on her. If she cared anything about you, she would be here taking caring of you.

I walked over to the dresser and picked up Ciara's wedding ring. "Oh wifey has finally learned to move on." I slid her ring on my finger. "It looks so much better on my finger instead."

"Kayla, what the fuck is wrong with you?! Take off her ring and get the hell out of here!" Smooth tried to get up, but hit his foot on the corner of the bed. "Shit!" He said grabbing his foot in pain.

I ran over to help him and beginning rubbing his foot. "Let me help you take the pain away." I rubbed and massaged his foot. I started sucking his toes. "I bet she doesn't do this, does she?" I continued to suck on his toes and Smooth didn't stop me. I got up and removed my dress and underwear.

"Let me show you how much I miss you." I said.

"Hurry up and show me." Smooth pulled down his gym shorts.

His dick popped out and I started kissing, licking, and sucking on it like it was the last dick on earth.

Ciara

I was finished and all done with stocking the new inventory. I had a little time to spare, so I took a break. I told London that I would be in my office if she needed me. Once I sat down, I called Smooth to check on him. Smooth's phone rang several times and went to voicemail. Maybe he's sleeping. So I called back again four more times. That was strange for Smooth not to answer his phone. He was a light sleeper so I knew that when I called him back to back that he would've woke up. I grabbed my purse and told London that I was going home to check on

Smooth. My boutique was in Oak Park and I lived in Westchester. It should take me about fifteen minutes.

I pulled up and noticed a white Jeep was parked in front of my house. I went inside and seen that Smooth's cellphone was on the couch. He must be upstairs I thought to myself. From the sound of the television, I knew that he was upstairs watching 300. As I got closer, I could hear moans from a woman. Maybe someone was having sex in the movie, so I didn't pay that no mind. Once I walked in our bedroom, I couldn't believe what I was seeing. Kayla was naked and riding my husband's dick in our bed. Smooth had his hands on her ass and was bouncing her up and down.

"Smooth, how could you!?" I pulled my gun out of my purse.

Smooth pushed Kayla off of him. "Ciara, I can explain!" Smooth said.

Pow! I shot Smooth in his leg. I pointed the gun at Kayla and pulled the trigger again but lucky for her the gun jammed.

Kayla started laughing and launched at me knocking the gun on the floor. We both fell to the floor and started wrestling. Kayla was on top of me. **Smack!** "Bitch, I'm wifey now." Kayla showed off my wedding ring that was on her finger. I kicked her off of me causing her to fall to the floor. Quickly, I grabbed the scissors off of my dresser and cut that bitch's finger off.

"Ahhhhh!" Kayla screamed in pain.

Smooth was yelling at me to stop. I threw the scissors at him and grabbed Kayla by her hair. I dragged

Kayla down my stairs. She's screaming and crying. "Bitch, shut the fuck up!" I punched her in her mouth. I opened my front door and could hear police sirens. I dragged Kayla down my front porch and tossed her naked ass on my lawn. Kayla just laid down in the grass crying. I went back inside to find Smooth pleading with me. I could hear the police outside now. I sat down on my living room couch and waited for them to enter my home.

Aftermath

Kelly and Anthony

Kelly and Anthony had a great big wedding and got married. Unfortunately six months later, GG died from complications of diabetes but she was blessed to see her only granddaughter get married. Kelly and her brother Shawn took it hard and became closer with their mother in prison. Kelly went back to school to receive her (MBA) Master of Business Administration and (MRED) Master's Degree in Real Estate Development. She started her own Real Estate Company called Global Real Estate. She later had a girl and a boy named, Jasmine and Justin.

Aaliyah and Vell

Aaliyah and Vell stayed together and worked everything out. Aaliyah went back to school and later on became an Interior Decorator. Ready for change, she and Vell relocated and moved to Atlanta. Aaliyah became a successful Interior Decorator and Vell eventually married her. Vell still remained a drug dealer and opened up several businesses.

Denise and Red

Denise and Neicy got married. Niecy had In Vitro Fertilization and had quadruplets. Two girls named, Raven and Rhianna. Two boys named, Jayden and Jordan. She owned two Day Care Centers, one on the Westside and Southside of Chicago. Red opened up several businesses of his own. A Moving Company, Car Lot, and a Restaurant.

Tia and Tommy

Tia and Tommy remained together. Tommy survived the shooting and had to do one year of rehabilitation. Tia stood by Tommy's side throughout it all. Tia's 'Teach Me How Too Strip Videos' put her on the map. She made half a million dollars off DVD sales and opened up several dance studios in different states. Tommy asked her to marry him because she remained by his side and Tia said yes. Tia had one daughter named, Royalty.

Ebony and Rio

Ebony was found dead in the trap house. Her mother identified her body at the morgue. Her murder was never solved. Her mother raised her daughter, Kimora.

Her cousin Rio was later found, killed a year later. They cut off his head and mailed it back to his mother in Chicago. The rest of his body was never found.

Kayla and Cherish

Kayla went to jail for Breaking and Entering, but got right out. She was still crazy in love with Smooth but he wasn't dealing with her. Kayla and Cherish were making money and eventually The Feds caught up with them. Kayla is now serving five years in a Federal Prison. Her daughter Variyah now lives with Smooth's mother.

Cherish copped a plea and told on her boyfriend Lorenzo. Cherish is now serving seven years and Lorenzo is now serving ten years in Federal Prison.

Smooth

Smooth became one of the biggest hustlers in Chicago. He stalked Ciara to the point that she had to put a restraining order against him. He never married or fell in love again. Smooth had a vasectomy making sure that he never had any more children. Smooth, Ant, Red, and Vell are still friends. Smooth opened up several business.

Ciara

Ciara and Smooth got a divorce. She got the house and through the help of Kelly, she sold it. One year later, she moved to Arizona and married Kanye. Unfortunately, Erica couldn't move with her because she wasn't allowed to do it legally. Erica lived with Smooth's mother. Ciara and Mrs. Jackson arranged for Erica to visit every summer. She went in partnership with London leaving her to run Bella Boutique in Chicago. She opened several boutiques in Arizona. Kanye took care of her and had a six bedroom home built from the ground up and bought her mother a home in Chicago too. Ciara was deeply in love with Kanye and finally had a baby girl. She named her daughter, Kenya. They both lived happily ever after.

CPSIA information can be obtained
at www.ICGtesting.com
Printed in the USA
LVOW04s1747021216

515533LV00010B/895/P